*"Thank you for helping me,
Mr. Valentine. You're obviously
a...very nice man."*

"Making those kinds of assumptions about a man
on such short acquaintance could be dangerous,
Ms. Pruitt. I'd advise against it in the future."

April quickly pulled her hand away from him,
looking down at it as if she hadn't realized she'd
even touched him.

"How much do you know about eighteen-month-
old boys?" he asked.

"Oh, well, I—actually, I'm afraid I don't know
anything at all. Why, do you have some?"

"Not yet," he said, wondering what the heck he
was going to do. "But I will soon."

This was never going to work, Dylan thought.
And then he stepped up to the counter to pay for
the purchase of April Pruitt and wondered how she
would feel about the fact that he needed her with
him twenty-four hours a day.

Dear Reader,

What makes readers love Silhouette Romance? Fans who have sent mail and participated on our www.eHarlequin.com community bulletin boards say they enjoy the heart-thumping emotion, the noble strength of the heroines, the truly heroic nature of the men—all in a quick yet satisfying read. I couldn't have said it better!

This month we have some fantastic series for you. Bestselling author Lindsay McKenna visits use with *The Will To Love* (SR 1618), the latest in her thrilling cross-line adventure MORGAN'S MERCENARIES: ULTIMATE RESCUE. Jodi O'Donnell treats us with her BRIDGEWATER BACHELORS title, *The Rancher's Promise* (SR 1619), about sworn family enemies who fight the dangerous attraction sizzling between them.

You must pick up *For the Taking* (SR 1620) by Lilian Darcy. In this A TALE OF THE SEA, the last of the lost royal siblings comes home. And if that isn't dramatic enough, in Valerie Parv's *Crowns and a Cradle* (SR 1621), part of THE CARRAMER LEGACY, a struggling single mom discovers she's a princess!

Finishing off the month are Myrna Mackenzie's *The Billionaire's Bargain* (SR 1622)—the second book in the latest WEDDING AUCTION series—about a most tempting purchase. And *The Sheriff's 6-Year-Old Secret* (SR 1623) is Donna Clayton's tearjerker.

I hope you enjoy this month's selection. Be sure to drop us a line or visit our Web site to let us know what we're doing right—and any particular favorite topics you want to revisit. Happy reading!

Mary-Theresa Hussey

Mary-Theresa Hussey
Senior Editor

Please address questions and book requests to:
Silhouette Reader Service
U.S.: 3010 Walden Ave., P.O. Box 1325, Buffalo, NY 14269
Canadian: P.O. Box 609, Fort Erie, Ont. L2A 5X3

The Billionaire's Bargain

Myrna Mackenzie

SILHOUETTE *Romance*

Published by Silhouette Books

America's Publisher of Contemporary Romance

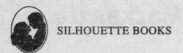

SILHOUETTE BOOKS

ISBN 0-373-19622-9

THE BILLIONAIRE'S BARGAIN

Copyright © 2002 by Myrna Topol

Visit Silhouette at www.eHarlequin.com

Printed in U.S.A.

Books by Myrna Mackenzie

Silhouette Romance

The Baby Wish #1046
The Daddy List #1090
Babies and a Blue-Eyed Man #1182
The Secret Groom #1225
The Scandalous Return of
  Jake Walker #1256
Prince Charming's Return #1361
Simon Says... Marry Me! #1429
At the Billionaire's Bidding #1442
Contractually His #1454
The Billionaire Is Back #1520
Blind-Date Bride #1526
A Very Special Delivery #1540
Bought by the Billionaire #1610
The Billionaire's Bargain #1622

*The Wedding Auction

Silhouette Books

Montana Mavericks
Just Pretending

Lone Star Country Club
Her Sweet Talkin' Man

MYRNA MACKENZIE,

winner of the Holt Medallion honoring outstanding
literary talent, believes that there are many unsung
heroes and heroines living among us, and she loves to
write about such people. She tries to inject her charac-
ters with humor, loyalty and honor, and after many
years of writing she is still thrilled to be able to say that
she makes her living by daydreaming. Myrna lives with
her husband and two sons in the suburbs of Chicago.
During the summer she likes to take long walks, and
during cold Chicago winters she likes to *think* about taking long walks (or dream of summers in Maine).
Readers may write to Myrna at P.O. Box 225,
LaGrange, IL 60525, or they may visit her online at
www.myrnamackenzie.com.

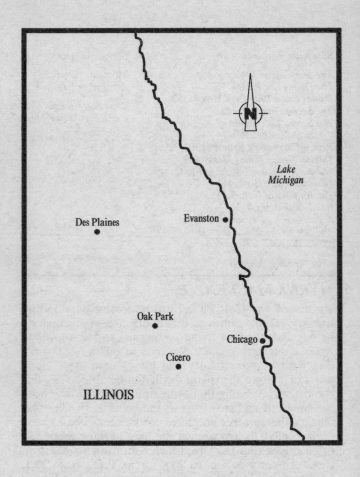

Chapter One

What *was* that woman doing behind that tree? Dylan Valentine craned his neck and caught a glimpse of curly blond hair and a slender form as the lady in question peeped out from behind the trunk of an old oak. Unfortunately, the woman looked up at that moment and caught him staring at her. Blushing prettily, she popped back bchind the tree.

Intriguing, Dylan thought, although it didn't really matter. She wasn't the type that he'd come here for. "Much too fragile for what I have in mind," he mumbled to himself.

"What did you say?" his friend Spencer asked. The Suburban Chicago Job Auction for Charity was in full swing in this green, leafy park, and Spencer and Dylan were here to find employees. Their friend, Ethan, had already made his choice and was somewhere on the grounds getting acquainted with the lady.

"I said that I need someone more like this one," Dylan said, showing Spencer a picture in the auction's brochure. "Someone hefty with a lot of stamina. I need an older woman, preferably one made of steel."

Spencer chuckled. "Dylan, I thought your stepmother said that she needed you to baby-sit your eighteen-month-old half brothers, not the Chicago Bears."

Dylan gave his friend a pained look. "Spence, I am a thirty-year-old bachelor. Do I look like a man who knows what to do with two…little people?"

Spencer grinned slightly. "Well, you've certainly had any number of women wanting to find out."

Dylan rubbed his jaw. "You know, maybe you're right. I probably am making too much of this situation. Besides, I suppose I could always get Uncle Spence to lend me a hand if I wander into deep water." He gave his friend a wicked grin.

Spencer laughed, holding up his hands in a defensive stance. "Okay, you win. I wouldn't want to be in your shoes, but do you really think this woman can solve your problems?" He glanced down at the somewhat muscular woman in the brochure.

"I'm counting on it," Dylan said. "Because left in the care of only their big half brother, I fear for the survival of the Valentine twins and the Valentine name. So I guess I'd better go check this kindergarten teacher out. I want her installed in my house by tonight before the boys arrive. Then I can relax."

But as he left his friend and headed off toward the area where the crowd was gathered, Dylan was anything but relaxed. He hadn't been since his stepmother, Vivian, had called. As he crossed the green, he glanced out the corner of his eye and saw the fragile blond woman peer from behind her tree again. She smiled at a group of women passing by, vacated her hiding place and slipped into their midst as they moved across the park toward the stage.

Dylan tilted his head, wondering at her behavior. Surrounded by a large group of chattering women, the lady was just as invisible as she'd been behind the tree.

"What an odd woman," he muttered to himself. On an impulse, he flipped through his brochure. April Pruitt. Another teacher, but this time from high school. No experience with little males with high voices. Not what he was looking for at all.

"Too delicate. No muscle." And anyway, he really didn't have time to wonder about the woman or her strange behavior. The kindergarten teacher might be auctioned off at any time. He struck out across the park once again, toward the women for sale in their summer dresses and business suits. Ah, there was the woman he was looking for. Agnes something. Very stern and capable-looking, solid. No doubt she'd know what to do with his half brothers when they arrived. He certainly didn't have a clue, something he'd tried to tell Vivian.

Dylan had been determined not to take the boys, he'd only ever seen them once or twice in their entire lives, but Vivian had wanted them to be with family. And now he was in desperate need of Agnes and her ability to handle beings under three feet tall.

Most of the candidates here today only wanted part-time positions. She was the only woman here who seemed promising.

Well, promising in the right way, Dylan thought, his gaze wandering to the group of women who'd been concealing his sprite. She had just stepped from the shelter of their midst.

Very attractive, he thought. In an ethereal way. Slight and slim, her dusty blond hair fell in curling layers to kiss her cheeks and throat and swished against her shoulders. A pale yellow floral dress hinted at gentle curves beneath, and floated around pretty legs encased in cream-colored stockings and shoes. She had a pair of little gold glasses hanging on a golden cord around her neck, and she looked pale and translucently lovely, a woman from a time long past.

She also looked just the tiniest bit like a woman trying to be braver than she really was.

Dylan wondered why, but as he watched her, she took a visibly deep breath, purposefully pushed her shoulders back, stepped up on the risers at center stage, and he finally noticed what he hadn't seen before.

There was a man staring at her. Intently. More like leering, really. He looked like he'd been waiting for this moment. His gaze followed her. He wanted the sprite…badly.

She didn't look even vaguely happy about the situation. If anything, she was avoiding eye contact with the man. And those shoulders were held rigid, her chin was stiff with determination. He knew that look. And he knew what it meant, though years had passed since he'd had personal experience of the emotions that triggered it. It was the look of someone who felt she had to be brave to protect herself.

"Dylan?"

Dylan whipped his head around, frowning. Spence and Ethan, who was still apparently waiting to finish his transaction, had come up behind him.

"She's not the kindergarten teacher," Spencer mused. "No muscles."

"She's not the one," Dylan agreed.

"Lovely though," Ethan speculated. "In a subtle sort of way."

"She isn't the one," Dylan repeated.

"Oh, I know that." Spencer looked toward the stage. "She doesn't look like she can handle a football team, but...very nice. You don't think she's pretty?"

Dylan raised one brow and continued to watch the man leering at the sprite. She started to take a step back, then held her ground.

"Dylan?" Spencer asked. "She's *not* the one, is she?"

"Of course not."

"Because," Ethan said, "although she *is* very appealing, that man...well, this does look somewhat private. They appear to know each other, Dylan," Ethan warned quietly. "Care to help Spencer find a likely candidate to hire? I don't think he's decided yet. At least, nothing's settled."

Dylan almost smiled at this obvious attempt to lead him away from the stage. Ethan and Spencer weren't his brothers, but there were times when they came close. Having been born to wealthy divorced parents who seemed to have wished they'd never had a child and who had regularly passed him around from reluctant relative to even more reluctant relative, Dylan had never gotten close to too many people until he met Spencer and Ethan in college. But the three of them had bonded almost instantly, and even during those times of the year when he was constantly traveling on business, he made a point of checking in with them on a regular basis. He knew them well, and so he knew that they'd try their best to protect him if they saw him running full tilt toward a brick wall.

"Don't worry," he said, shaking his head. "I'm not particularly interested in the lady," he repeated.

Spencer coughed.

Okay, so his friends were right. The lady on the risers *did* interest him, Dylan admitted. But the reasons she snagged his attention were all wrong. The buttons she was pushing were personal. And best forgotten.

He wanted to turn away and go with his friends. He even *started* to turn away. Then he looked at her again. Even from this distance, he could see that she was struggling to smile at the audience. He took a step closer to the stage.

"You two have things to do. Go do them," he told his friends.

For a few seconds, neither of them moved. They knew him too well to simply dismiss this situation. In an attempt to emphasize his need to take care of business, Dylan moved forward across the grass closer to the stage. His friends followed.

He let out a sigh. "All right then, what do you expect me to do? He's a predator. Look," he ordered, and together Ethan and Spencer glanced toward the man who was now crowding close to the stage, a smug look on his face as he waited to buy an obviously unhappy April Pruitt.

Dylan glanced over his shoulder at his friends, waiting.

Seconds passed.

"It's just a formality, no more," he said. "I'm still bidding on the kindergarten teacher. I'm not hiring this one, but I can't just walk away. You understand why? I..."

He didn't need to finish. They knew his past.

"All right," Spence finally said after exchanging a look with Ethan. "If you insist, we'll go, but be careful."

"I always am. In all things," Dylan agreed, feeling

his friends walk away, but never taking his eyes off the woman. Her face was a pale, pretty oval, her lips pressed together tightly in that pasted on smile. Her stance was slightly rigid, her body in its old-fashioned dress looking as if it might break with any physical contact. And as he drew closer, Dylan saw that her eyes were a rich, deep violet. She stared resolutely at the auctioneer except when that man, that very large man who was ogling her, placed a bid on her. Then her eyes flickered, her head jerked. But she held the smile and the mock-brave stance.

"Well, well, well, April. Almost done." The big man's voice was raspy, chilly. He had the look of a man who'd grown up grinding the wings of butterflies beneath his heel. "Just let me get rid of my competition," he added. "Then it'll just be you and me. At last."

Dylan thought he imagined a tremor shimmy through the pretty woman's body. Her skin seemed to grow even paler. In the next instant, she lifted her chin high.

Defiance. She even managed to broaden her phony smile and hold it for a few seconds.

Admiration flowed through Dylan at the lady's unexpectedly bold move.

"It won't be just you and me, Jason," the woman said quietly. "I'll match your bid and donate the money myself."

The man chuckled. "Oh, I don't think you will. I've got more money than you can spare on a teacher's salary. Let's just make that bid five thousand dollars."

The auctioneer shifted uncomfortably, but he called out the man's bid. Then he glanced over to the last person who'd made a counter-bid. "I've got five thousand. Do I hear fifty-five hundred?"

The elderly potential bidder looked at the man who

was glaring at him threateningly. Sadly the old man shook his head.

"Five thousand. Five thousand once." The auctioneer's voice was a quiet stab in the silence that had settled in.

"Fifty-five hundred," the young woman said, though her voice shook.

Dylan swore beneath his breath. She'd already offered her time for the summer and now she was being forced to bid on herself, money she probably couldn't afford. All because some man several times her size was doing his best to scare her.

The big man chuckled again, a cold, oily sound. "Six thousand, you witch."

The woman's delicate features looked strained, but, taking a deep, shaky breath, she opened her mouth.

"Ten." Dylan's voice was low and sounded much calmer than he felt.

The big man turned with a lurching jerk. "What'd you say, mister?"

He'd said something he no doubt shouldn't have said since he had no intention of hiring this woman, however pretty she might be. And since, as he had reminded Spencer and Ethan, he'd known a few bullies himself when he was very young, times like this brought back memories he didn't care to resurrect. Still, there was no turning back now. And this *was* a good cause. He could well afford to simply donate the money.

Dylan raised one brow as he gazed at the man. Then he smiled slightly and walked closer to his opponent. The man was big, fully two-hundred-fifty-plus pounds to Dylan's one-ninety, but Dylan's six-three frame topped his. The man's hands, however, were a different story. Thick and broad, they looked like they were made for hitting, and he very definitely was itching to hit something—most likely Dylan—with great force.

Glancing up toward the platform, Dylan gave the woman a slight nod and a reassuring smile. She was not, however, looking relieved.

He turned to the auctioneer. "I said ten thousand," he repeated, as if it had been the auctioneer and not the threatening bidder who had asked the question.

The auctioneer smiled broadly. "Ten thousand it is. Ten thousand once. Ten thousand twice."

"Eleven thousand." The other man raised his voice. Dylan turned to the side, to see that his opponent's face was blotched with red.

"You really should see a doctor about your stress levels," he said quietly. "I'll raise my bid to twenty-five thousand."

"You're nuts, buddy," the man said. "Totally, damn nuts. She's not worth *that* much. No woman is, and this one is worse than most. Too many brains, too straitlaced and too opinionated and outspoken for her own good, if you ask me."

Dylan glanced up to where the slender woman stood watching what was happening below her. She was holding herself very still as if to control her emotions. Suddenly she smiled at him, just a small smile really, but he felt as if a rainbow had passed through his heart. It was such an unexpected and totally unwelcome sensation that Dylan nearly took a step back.

He forced himself to smile slightly.

"Ah, brains and strong opinions? Is that so?" he asked, trying to steer the conversation into lighter waters now that he was on the verge of winning her freedom.

To his surprise, this little shivering slip of a woman nodded. "Well, I'm afraid the strong opinion part is especially true. I don't always follow the road most traveled. You probably should know that." Her voice was clear and musical.

Not that any of that mattered, Dylan thought, since he wasn't really going to hire her.

And neither was the other guy. He glanced toward the man still standing there, clenching and unclenching his hands.

"Twenty-five thousand. Going, going…"

"I could continue this, and I would, but I wouldn't want her to get the wrong idea and think it mattered that much. Besides, I've had my fun today, and you'll be sorry," the man warned, narrowing his eyes at Dylan.

Somewhere in the background, the auctioneer said, "gone."

And the air nearly slipped out of the woman's body. Her knees buckled for half a second before she caught herself and straightened.

Nevertheless and without much thought, Dylan moved forward and up onto the stage. He carefully eased an arm around her shoulders. "You're all right?" he asked quietly.

For a few long seconds she didn't move as he gazed down at the pale crest of her hair. Then she breathed in deeply and looked up at him.

"I'm…yes, I'm fine. Thank you. How—how totally silly of me." And she disentangled herself from his grasp. She looked down to where the other man still stood.

"I hope he makes you earn every penny," Jason snarled. "She won't make a good employee," he told Dylan. "You'll probably have to bring her down a peg or two. Or three." And he stomped away through the long grass.

Dylan looked down at the slender woman standing by his side and together they left the stage and began to walk away. "Thank you," she said in a voice like warm scented water pouring over him. "Jason and I, well, we have our differences."

He tilted his head toward where he assumed the group of teachers stood behind them now. "You should stay in a group. With your friends."

"For the record," she said, "I don't think he would have physically harmed me. Jason deals more in verbal abuse. He's upset because I once knew a teacher who'd dated him and, based on her bad experience and the scientific likelihood of such a thing happening again, I turned him down repeatedly when he asked me out. I don't think he's used to hearing 'no' very much. I suspect he would have taken great pleasure in being able to have some control over me for a short time, but... I don't think he would go beyond that. It would have been illogical to do so. Jason is an attorney. Beating up a teacher might have harmed his business. I don't think he's actually violent."

"I don't know about that, but even verbal abuse can be terrible," Dylan said as they walked farther afield. "You still need to be careful around someone like him." He gazed down into those wide, violet eyes that spoke of innocence.

"I'm not as naive as I look," she said, with a sudden smile, as if she'd read his mind. "And I'm always careful. For the record, Mr...."

"Valentine."

Those eyes widened a bit more. "What a nice name. And as I was saying, I'm very careful. Extremely practical. I teach mathematics and science."

"Well then," he said, his voice swooping low. "If

you're practical, I hope you can take as well as give advice. Do all that you can to steer clear of the man.''

She touched his arm then, her slender fingers resting on his sleeve, warming him through the cloth. As if she hadn't just gone through a threatening experience with a man. Oh yeah, she could say she wasn't naive, but the facts were plain enough. This one has no real sense of preservation, Dylan thought. Thank goodness she hadn't been hired by some man who could read her too easily and would take advantage. As it was, she hadn't been hired at all. She was free to go her own way.

"Thank you for helping me, Mr. Valentine," she said. "You're obviously a very nice man."

"Making those kinds of assumptions about a man on such short acquaintance could be dangerous, Ms. Pruitt. I'd advise against it in future." He looked down to where her delicate fingers still rested on his sleeve. For one mad second, he thought of how innocent that touch was and just how insane it could make a man if she dragged those fingertips across his bare chest. Instantly, he reared back from the sensations his runaway thoughts had called up. He frowned.

As if his disapproving expression had burned her, she quickly pulled her hand away, looking down at it as if she hadn't realized that she'd even touched him. From the pretty blush that colored her skin, Dylan could guess that she hadn't, and he nearly groaned. April Pruitt was obviously one of those impulsive innocent touchers, the kind of women some men just loved to take advantage of.

Not that that was his problem. He was done here, wasn't he?

"Well, Ms. Pruitt, I'll see you around," he said. "Take care."

For a moment she looked confused. Then she suddenly smiled. "Oh yes, you must be wanting to stay and watch the rest of the auction. All right then. I'll meet up with you here when the auction is over, and you can explain my duties to me then." She turned to go, but at that moment, the auctioneer called out "sold." Drawn by the sound, Dylan turned just in time to see Agnes Mason, his eminently suitable kindergarten teacher being escorted away by the winning bidder.

He wanted to yell "no," to turn back time.

Instead, he did what he always did. He made do with the situation at hand.

"Wait. Don't leave. Ms. Pruitt, how much do you know about eighteen-month-old boys?" he asked.

She turned back to him, opening her eyes wide. "Oh, well, actually, I'm afraid I don't know anything at all. Why, do you have some?"

"Not yet," he said, wondering what the heck he was going to do. "But I will soon."

The lady blinked, her eyes wide. She almost looked like a child herself.

This was never going to work, Dylan thought. And then he stepped over to the counter to pay for the purchase of April Pruitt.

He wondered how she would feel about the fact that he needed her with him twenty-four hours a day.

Chapter Two

"Oh, no. Babies. Sweet little chubby-cheeked babies with tiny wobbly chins and angelic eyes and…oh, even worse, a man like the ones my mother always warned me about, a wildly gorgeous man with eyes like sunset. I absolutely cannot do this. How did I ever, ever, ever let this happen? Wasn't I paying attention? Wasn't my brain functioning?" April Pruitt whispered to herself as she parked her car in front of Dylan Valentine's imposing manor home a few hours later.

Something had gone very wrong at the auction today. She was supposed to have been presented as a perfect candidate to tutor students in math and science, or someone who could set up databases or manage financial records. But something had happened—Jason Olney and Dylan Valentine had happened—and now here she was, about to face the babies, and the man. It was just the sort of situation she'd sworn she'd avoid after her "big mistake." Maybe her mother was right. Maybe she was destined to relive the worst parts of her family's history.

April rested her head on the steering wheel and groaned, wondering how she could have allowed all this to happen. Back at the auction, in a whirl of information that she had barely registered, Dylan had briefly explained that he was having some unexpected company and he would need her as a round-the-clock baby-sitter. When the auction organizers had checked Dylan out, he'd turned out to be the genuine article and a major benefactor to Safe House.

"So, heck, what else could I have done, anyway?" Safe House was just too darn important. The charity had helped one of her students who used to live in the city escape the tragedy of ending up in a gang. The organization had kept him off the streets and given him a chance, so there was no way she could ever turn away from a donation the size of Dylan Valentine's. There hadn't been any alternative, so in the end, she'd packed her bags and come along to his house, prepared to fulfill her end of the bargain she'd made with Dylan. But now...

"I don't know the first thing about toddlers," she whispered as she climbed out of her car and made her way to the imposing front door. There were really good reasons for that, too. Ones she didn't want to think about. She also didn't want to think about how attractive her new boss was.

But attractive was too mild a word to describe Dylan, April concluded as he opened the front door to let her in. What she saw made her stomach flip over with distress. Dark brown hair tousled just enough to make a woman want to touch, sleepy amber eyes, broad shoulders. In a white shirt and black pants he towered over her, looking like an invitation to sin, or fantasize. Or maybe to panic if you were the type of woman who happened to run from fantasies.

I'm the type, April thought.

Still, she gave Dylan a weak smile.

He smiled back—just barely—and her heart did some sort of silly leaping thing. She closed her eyes in distress. Hadn't she already traveled this path and lived to regret it?

"I can't do this," she said, and then opened her eyes, realizing that she'd actually said the words out loud. She clapped one hand over her mouth. "I'm so sorry," she whispered. After all, the man had saved her from Jason's wrath, he'd donated twenty-five thousand dollars to a cause she treasured.

To her surprise, his lips tilted up in a half smile. "Don't feel too bad. I was thinking the same thing myself."

Her eyes opened wider. Maybe she'd get a reprieve. "I can leave if you'd like."

He chuckled. "Don't even think it. In less than three hours, my stepmother will be here with my baby brothers, and I wouldn't begin to trust myself to take care of them alone." Reaching down, he took her bag and drew her into the house.

Okay, so it had been stupid to hope he'd change his mind. April looked around her and stepped gingerly into the huge hallway with its wide curling mahogany staircase. She lifted the gold glasses that hung on a chain around her neck and perched them on her nose so that she could get a better view of her temporary home. Sunlight played on the black-and-white marble tile and bounced off the portraits of what had to be a long line of Valentine ancestors, all staring somewhat sternly down at her. They probably knew she didn't belong here.

"Wow, this doesn't exactly look like nursery material," she said. "Not that I'd know," she quickly added, shoving away the thought of another unused nursery, another time.

Dylan's laugh was a deep, low, purely male sound. "I suppose you're right. It's been a great many years since I was a boy, and no one young has lived here since then. Not that I'd know what nursery material is, either. I suppose we'll learn together, Ms. Pruitt."

"Oh, call me April. I'm not all that comfortable with my last name. I'm thinking of changing it soon, anyway."

Dylan blinked at that, but didn't ask what she meant. Which was probably just as well. People always thought her a bit odd when she told them about her plans to scientifically locate the perfect, intellectually suited mate for herself. In fact, her goal was almost within her reach now, she hoped.

Still, having thrown out that statement, April figured she should at least explain herself. "When I was young, the boys used to change my last name to 'Prude.' It seems to have stuck in my mind like a bad jingle, and I can never quite forget it."

He nodded, a quick, brisk movement. "Yes, well, I understand what you mean. With a last name like Valentine, I've gotten my share of comments."

And with a face that matched his name, she'd just bet he had. His features were strong, hard and wickedly handsome, the kind of valentine most women dreamed of finding in their beds.

"Wh-when did you say your brothers would be arriving?" she asked suddenly, half-afraid that she might have whispered her thoughts out loud.

"Too soon," he said.

"You don't like your...brothers?" All right, she couldn't help stumbling over her words. "Mr. Valentine, if you don't mind my asking, just how old are you?"

Her question brought a grin to his face and a blush to her own. "I know, a thirty-year-old man with eighteen-month-old brothers, it boggles the mind, doesn't it? Let's just say that my father liked young wives, he had several and no, I don't dislike my brothers. I don't even know them. I'm just a bit nonplussed at being asked to care for them."

"You don't know your brothers?"

"We just never got acquainted. My father died more than a year ago."

She opened her mouth to say the polite thing, but he held his hand up. "Thank you, but we weren't close." His words were curt and didn't invite further discussion. "Anyway, as far as the reason for my stepmother asking, I can only guess that she thought he and I were closer than we were. *She* probably didn't even know my father all that well. She was his fifth wife, and he had a way of romancing a woman, marrying her and then getting out when things got too domestic. Usually as soon as she started to even think about having babies, which is why I don't have any other siblings besides these two. Somehow Vivian made it past that stage, but once she conceived, I doubt she saw much of her husband at all, and she only met me a few times."

April wondered what had happened between Dylan and his father, but that wasn't any of her business. And the less she speculated about the man, the better. "She wants you to take care of her children and she doesn't even know you very well?"

He shrugged. "Viv's thinking of getting married again, and she wants some time to get to know her fiancé better and make sure she's doing the right thing this time. I think she's scared of making the same mistake twice, but she refuses to leave her children with anyone but family. Unfortunately, she doesn't have any, and my father didn't have much. Just me and an elderly, baby-hating aunt. I don't relish this task. Family isn't exactly my forte, but I'd hate to see any child end up with the wrong father or my Aunt Nedra, so…'' He held out his hands in a gesture of surrender.

''You figured you couldn't do anything but accept your fate,'' she said softly, jarred by how closely the words had echoed her own thoughts just a few minutes earlier.

''Touché, April, there you have it.''

She couldn't help smiling, then. ''Those poor babies.''

He narrowed his eyes. ''I certainly don't intend to be an ogre just because I don't know them.''

April shook her head. ''No, I was just thinking of how little you and I appear to know about taking care of children. They should have better. I guess we'll just have to approach this logically, learn as much as we can as quickly as we can.''

''I agree. And thank you. I know this wasn't what you had in mind when you volunteered for the auction. I finally read all the details of your résumé. A minor in computer science and advanced degrees in both mathematics and biology.''

''I know, but what can I say? I grew up with my head stuffed full of mathematical equations, scientific and technobabble and my mother's axioms for achieving success in life. I had a professor in college who convinced me that I would enjoy the freedom of shaping young minds and sharing my knowledge more than I would like being enclosed in an office, and he was probably right. I *do* feel that I click with my students. I remember that awkwardness and self-consciousness of my teens, so I feel honor-bound to guide them as much as I can through the terrible emotional highs and lows of that age. Every day of teaching high school is a challenge and an adventure, and I take great joy in the kids I work with.

"But teenagers aren't anything like toddlers," she reminded him solemnly. "They're not anything like any other age as far as I can tell, so just because I'm good with them doesn't mean a thing here, I'm afraid. In fact, I've heard other teachers say that you're either good at relating to older kids or to younger ones, but rarely both. And I tend to feel as if I was born a teenager. My mother certainly always treated me like one, and not only I have zero experience with babies, I somehow even missed the playing-with-dolls phase of my childhood. Too bad. It might have come in handy right now."

He lifted one dark brow. "Maybe, but I suspect Jordie and Sam are a bit more demanding than dolls might be."

"Well, I guess we'll find out what we're up against soon enough." She braced herself for what was to come. "Three hours you said?"

"Umm. Or maybe a little less now."

"Of course. Less." His words made everything suddenly real. In less than three hours, babies would come into her life. Deep panic began to assault her. She fought it by looking up into Dylan's eyes. A mistake.

She was pretty sure those dark amber eyes had witnessed many women at close range and in intimate situations. Gazing up at Dylan this way, it was obvious that he could easily seduce a woman into doing things she knew would change her life—maybe forever—in ways that might hurt her irrevocably. She'd already been seduced that way once.

April nearly jumped back a step.

Heavens, she was caught in a dilemma. Think about the babies or think about this stunning, unnervingly masculine man? Which was less unsettling?

"Let me show you the house so you can get your bearings before they arrive," Dylan suddenly said, saving her from her own thoughts. His voice had been gentle. For half a second, she thought she saw concern on his face. Did he think she couldn't handle the situation or had he read the panic in her expression? Surely he didn't know how he was affecting her?

"Yes, I'd like that," she said, as if gulping a deep drink of water. She followed him down the hallway.

The huge red-brick Georgian was beautiful, with large rooms and massive furniture. Lots of dark woodwork. In the room where Dylan anticipated letting the boys sleep, April fingered the heavy hunter-green drapes and noted the maroon wallpaper.

"There's a delivery arriving any minute. Beds and whatever else the store thinks we might need. Do you think you can do something with this room?"

Oh no, he wanted her to decorate. She, who barely paid attention to the fact that she *had* furniture in her house. But this was a job, not her life.

"I can do something," she agreed, determined to at least try. "I'm sure I can manage."

But could she? When for three years, she'd steered clear of anything that reminded her of babies? All her life she had struggled to prove she was a mature individual not as much like her grandmother as appearances suggested and yet, already, at only twenty-five, she had already made two of her grandmother's most major mistakes. Her emotions had been allowed to rule her. She'd fallen for the wrong man. Then she'd made things even worse by getting pregnant, ending up alone and losing the child. Was this a sign of a woman who could manage a difficult and demanding situation?

"I don't have the experience, but I'm very determined to succeed, Mr. Valentine." April raised her chin.

"Call me Dylan."

She looked into his eyes. And she was very afraid that all the determination in the world wouldn't save a woman like her in a situation like this.

Dylan Valentine was an obvious heartbreaker. Any woman with an operative brain would get out of here fast, and she was reputed to have more than her share of gray matter. But he was in a bind. He needed her help to give two babies a few weeks of security and attention rather than ship them off to a baby-hating aunt. How could she let him down?

She couldn't, and that alone was enough to let her know what a precarious situation this was. She'd known the man all of ten minutes, and already she was unable to say "no." That fact didn't bode well for what was to come.

Well, what was an intelligent woman to do in such a situation? Who knew? They didn't teach those things in school, but she figured that the next time Dylan glanced at her, and those sexy, I'd-love-to-find-you-in-my-bed-sweetheart eyes made her breath catch in her throat, she was going to improvise. If she could do nothing else to chase him from her thoughts, she could at least recite mathematical formulas in her head.

It was a less than satisfactory solution, but she was a desperate woman. Besides, she knew an awful lot of mathematical formulas. April figured she was going to need every single one of them during the next three weeks if she was going to play house with Dylan.

Dylan had to admit that April was a determined woman. Every time he said the word "baby," she blanched, but she didn't stop working. Not for a second. For two hours after all the supplies arrived from Lullaby Village, she had been hanging curtains, smoothing tiny sheets onto tiny beds, filling the drawers of the dressers with miniature articles of clothing, placing toys in the turquoise and yellow toy bins and directing him in the placement of a mobile. Several times when he'd accidentally looked directly into those pretty violet eyes, he could have sworn he heard her whispering the Pythagorean theorem and murmuring something about Cantor's theory of transfinite numbers, but that might have simply been his own overly fertile imagination. April Pruitt might have been called a prude by boys too young to know better, she might sneak those prissy little gold glasses onto her nose now and then, she might know more about such dry subjects as math and computers than most of his employees, but there was something achingly feminine about her. And it was messing with his head.

Which was too damn bad, because he didn't like having his head messed with, and he definitely didn't like not being in control of all his responses with women.

This one, however, had him puzzled. She was smart, she was visibly determined to be strong, and yet there was something tremendously vulnerable about her, which he was pretty sure he wasn't supposed to notice. He didn't want to notice it, either.

Furthermore, she was positively petrified at the thought of his little brothers. No matter what she said or did, she couldn't hide it, and he couldn't very well ignore it. He'd hired her because *he* was uncomfortable at the thought of dealing with the boys.

"You're sure you're all right with this?" he asked, noticing the way April's fingers trembled slightly as she picked up a plastic container of baby powder that had somehow come open in the box. Breathing in the subtle scent, even Dylan couldn't associate it with anything other than innocence.

"Oh, sure, I'm fine," she said, with what might have passed as casual good cheer, except for the fact that her body was absolutely rigid.

Without planning to, Dylan brushed his fingers across her own. They were icy. The sliver of heat that passed through his body obviously didn't come from the lady. He raised one brow.

"Level with me, April."

She firmed her lips and looked directly into his eyes. "All right, if you level with me. Why exactly did you bid on me today? It was because of Jason, wasn't it?"

He frowned, but he didn't deny it.

"Be honest, was I the person you would have chosen to hire if he hadn't been there bothering me?"

Dylan wondered what the best answer to this would be. She was clearly upset about something, but one look in her eyes told him that she'd been lied to in the past and was worried about being lied to again.

"I was planning on bidding on a kindergarten teacher. Agnes something or other."

She nodded firmly. "Agnes Mason. Yes, I know her. We've met from time to time when the high school and grammar schools have joint teacher institution days. She's very motherly. She would have been good at this.

Perfect, actually. She would have loved living here, doing this.''

He almost smiled. ''And you won't? April, do you want to go back to the auction and try for someone else?''

That jolted those violet eyes wide. ''Of course not. You hired me. I'm here. You're donating your money to Safe House. Besides, the auction's over. I want to contribute, and you need someone. If it's not me, well, I think I can be better than your Aunt Nedra. I don't hate babies.''

''But you don't feel comfortable with them.''

''Well,'' she said with a little shrug. ''Maybe not yet, but I will. I'm sure that getting used to dealing with babies is like anything else. It just takes a bit of experience. Then you're in the groove and everything's fine.''

''So you're sure you want to stay with me?'' he asked, gazing down at her.

''Yes,'' she said, and her answer was barely a whisper. For a moment, Dylan forgot that they were talking about babies, and he thought they were discussing something else entirely. For half a second, he envisioned himself reaching out, placing his hands around her waist and dragging her body against his, tasting those soft pink lips beneath his.

Abruptly, he realized what was going through his head. He straightened and shoved one hand back through his hair.

''Well, um, yes, that's very good then,'' he said. ''In a few hours we'll be just fine, I'm sure.'' And he hoped she was right. This just took some getting used to.

Then everything would be routine and right.

And he would stop wanting to bed his brothers' babysitter.

Chapter Three

Had she really told Dylan that everything would be fine? Well, hey, she would just have to make sure that was true, April decided when the doorbell finally rang, signalling the boys' arrival.

"Dylan, love," a petite dark-haired woman cried, as he opened the door and she whooshed inside, pushing a stroller containing two little cherubs. "It's so good to see you, dear. You're a total lifesaver. Have I told you that?"

"Only about fifty times since you asked me to do this," Dylan said with a chuckle as he turned and motioned April to come closer.

"Well, it's only the truth. Yes, just put that down over there, Allen," Vivian said to the chauffeur, who was carrying in boxes and suitcases. "Oh, Dylan, I just don't know what I would have done if you hadn't agreed to take care of my dear loves." She beamed down at the two wide-eyed little boys seated in the stroller, then stepped around all the clutter and gave her stepson a hug.

"You know you only have to ask when you need something," Dylan told his stepmother, returning her hug and holding out a hand to April, luring her closer still. "Besides, I won't be doing this all on my own. I'd like you to meet April Pruitt. April has agreed to help me."

For a moment, Vivian blinked. She looked at April. "How nice. And April is…a friend?"

Vivian's worried frown implied that the only kind of female friends Dylan had were those he slept with. April felt her skin turning warm and pink.

"Only an employee." April hastily choked the words out. She tried not to notice that Dylan was grinning.

"An employee, Viv," he agreed. "And I'll thank you not to fluster her. April is doing me a favor. She's a teacher."

"Oh, well then," Vivian said, relief clear in her voice. She held out perfectly manicured hands to take April's own. "A professional to take care of my babies. How wonderful, Dylan! And thank you so much, April. I can't tell you how stressful it is to be leaving my children. We've never been apart. I'm so grateful that Dylan found someone qualified to help him with my precious angels. A teacher, what luck!"

And Vivian hugged April close as if they'd known each other forever rather than for less than a minute.

April liked the bubbly woman immediately, but gazing down at the two blue-eyed cuties in the stroller, she couldn't help wanting to explain the truth to Vivian.

April opened her mouth.

"Do you think they'll remember me when I get back?" Vivian asked suddenly.

And April decided then and there that she would say nothing more to worry Vivian. She would do her very best by these sweet-looking little boys, but she could not cause this mother more concern than she was already feeling. April closed her mouth.

She felt Dylan's hand at her back and looked up. He smiled slightly as if he'd known what she was about to do and approved of her decision to keep quiet.

"They'll remember you. Can you stay for a visit, Viv?" he asked.

He eyed the boys, and April was unsure whether he was just being hospitable or just stalling for time. Now that they were here in person, the babies seemed so real, so much more of a responsibility than they had seemed before.

"Guh," one of them said, holding up his arms.

"Yes, Sam, you remember your uncle Dylan, don't you, sweetheart?"

Sam jabbered to his brother, who took in his words with a solemn expression.

"I'm sorry, Dylan, but I really can't stay. I'm running late as it is, and Lawrence is meeting me at the airport. Unfortunately, I have to go very soon."

And she and Dylan would be left alone with these two needy little darlings, April thought. They would be responsible for the lives of these beautiful babies. A slight thread of panic slithered through her.

Apparently, she wasn't the only panicked person. "This is so, so hard," Vivian was saying. "I wanted to have more time to set things up with you, but as I told you the other day, Sam developed a cold, his ears were sensitive to air travel and we were held up. I wasn't sure I could even leave them at all. As it is, I have so many things you need to know, so much I need to tell you." And she proceeded to pull out a thick notebook with scribbled writing and to explain that Jordie needed to hear a lullaby at bedtime, but that Sam preferred a story, that Sam had a weakness for applesauce but that he shouldn't be allowed too much of it, that she had her itinerary outlined hour by hour and that they should call her at the least sign of trouble. The list of explanations went on and on, but finally Vivian's voice broke, and Dylan touched her hand.

"We'll read it," he promised.

Vivian nodded weakly. She turned toward her sons.

"Bye. Bye. Bye-bye," one little blue-eyed urchin chirped to his mother, answering her tearful cries and the kisses she was blowing him by flinging his tiny arms wide.

"Take care of them, please, Dylan," Vivian said. "They're my life, my world. Oh, do you think it's really right for me to go off and leave them this way? What if—"

"I'll guard them with my life, Viv," Dylan said firmly, gently. "I promise you. You know, you don't have to go if you don't want to, though. No one's forcing you to go, are they?"

April glanced up at that. There he went again, doing that protective male thing. She studied Dylan, the way his dark hair fell across his forehead, the angry concern in his voice.

"No, of course not. Lawrence is a perfect gentleman. I just— I don't want to make a mistake again, you know? I mean… It's not that your father was a mistake, exactly, but—"

"Don't apologize, Viv," Dylan said gently. "I know very well what my father was. And you're right to test the waters this time, but I promise I'll do my best with Jordie and Sam. That's why I hired April, you know."

April took a deep breath as Vivian turned dark worried eyes on her. She struggled for a calming smile.

"I'm sure the boys and I will have a good time, Mrs. Valentine, and I'll…I'll…" She would what? April searched for something that would be both feasible and offer reassurance when she herself was unsure about this situation. "I'll keep a computer log of their activities. I'll make a scrapbook. I'll take photos so you won't miss too many moments. I'll—"

"I think you can see that April will make sure you have a record of the next few weeks," Dylan cut in, saving her from making any more rash promises. It was just as well, April acknowledged. She hadn't been too sure what to say next. She'd wanted to promise the young worried mother that her children would have the same kind of expert care Agnes Mason would have provided, to comfort Vivian with lies.

Moments later, Vivian was finally heading out the door and April was the one feeling scared. "Oh, yes, I forgot, it's almost dinnertime," Vivian said, stopping in her tracks on her way to the door and turning toward Dylan and April. "The boys are used to eating at five o'clock. Their special meal is in the insulated bag I brought. And they like to take a bath after dinner and then go to bed and then…" Her voice trailed away as Dylan escorted her out to her car.

The room quickly filled with pregnant silence. Baby-scented silence.

For a moment April wanted to run after the two adults, but she forced herself to turn to the little boys and smile.

They smiled back.

"Buh," one of them said. April looked at the *S* on his shirt.

"How do you do, Sam?" she said, her voice coming out slightly choppy.

He laughed. She tried not to think that her own child would only have been a little over a year older than this, still cute, still cuddly and laughing with soft silky curls.

"And Jordie," she said to the much quieter, solemn-eyed little boy who reminded her a bit of Dylan. "Hi, sweetie."

He didn't smile but his eyes fixed on her, huge and intense and heartbreakingly liquid. His chin wobbled. "Ma," he said. He looked toward the door.

Oh no. Was he going to cry? What would she do if he cried? April thought, nearly ready to cry herself.

When she heard Dylan's steps coming through the door, it was all she could do not to turn, run past the boys and him and go home where she could lock herself away from this raw, scared feeling that was growing more intense.

Just breathe, she told herself, inhaling deeply, forcing herself to do it slowly. Just hold on. You'll get used to them. To the boys. To the man. You'll become numb soon, immune to the situation.

She turned to look at Dylan, and saw that he was eyeing her and the boys and tugging at his tie as if gearing up for some gargantuan task, like scaling the Himalayas...or getting to know his baby brothers. In spite of herself, she smiled.

"Not exactly your ordinary day, is it?" she asked.

He smiled. "Not quite like a day at the office, no."

It occurred to her that he had hired her in part because he *did* have an office to go to. She would be alone with the boys part of the time. Which might be for the best. One less male to worry about. And looking at Dylan's achingly broad chest and killer smile told her she should try to spend as few hours with him as possible. This was a topic she needed to pursue.

"You know what I do for a living. What type of office do you work in?" She noticed that Sam had gotten out of his chair and was starting to toddle around the room. Jordie was still wearing that lost look, and he was eyeing Dylan warily.

"I own a company that researches and installs the latest in advanced security systems. Mostly corporate, but we do some residential work as well."

"You'll want to return to work," she said softly, not wanting to sound too hopeful.

Dylan glanced at Sam as the little boy neared an electrical outlet. He scooped up the baby for barely two seconds and set him down elsewhere as if he didn't want to hold on to him. Then he looked down at April.

"Don't worry. I haven't taken any time off for a while. I can afford a few days here and there. I do a lot of traveling. In fact, when this adventure with the boys is over, I'm planning on leaving the country for a while to expand into some European locations. I have good people working for me. They know how to manage while I'm gone."

So he would be here. With her. She swallowed and nodded.

Suddenly Jordie started to cry.

April turned toward the little boy, her limbs frozen, her heart somersaulting. She glanced at Dylan, who suddenly looked big and male and more awkward than she had seen him all day.

Okay, so she was going to have to be the one to do this. She braced herself for her first contact with a baby in several years. Then she lurched forward.

She smacked hard into Dylan, who had also moved

forward and was holding his big hands out to Jordie. And suddenly those big hands were on her as she teetered on her feet. Catching her, keeping her from falling. Warm, capable hands. He smoothed them down her back and she nearly gasped. Then he steadied her and set her back on her feet. She looked up into Dylan's eyes.

"You're...all right?" he asked. "I didn't hurt you?"

She shook her head vehemently, wishing she could move away without looking so obvious, so much like a scared virginal type when she wasn't a virgin at all. She'd had her night of seduction—once. But she didn't want to think about that night...or Dylan's hands.

"Jordie," was all April managed to say and this time she stood back and let Dylan awkwardly lift the little boy. She was relieved when the startled toddler stopped crying and gazed straight into his big brother's eyes, momentarily silenced. At least *she* wouldn't have to stare straight into those eyes. And she didn't even know whether she meant Dylan's seductive ones or Jordie's heartbroken ones.

Instead, she reached down and picked up Sam, who was beginning to wander into forbidden territory again. Sam immediately shifted his attention to the entertainment at hand, his fingers. He didn't even seem to notice that he was being held, and that made April feel just a touch more in control of her emotions.

"We're going to the kitchen for dinner now," she announced firmly, needing activity. "After that, baths and bed."

"Ah, an organized woman, little brother," Dylan said, still holding Jordie three feet away from his body as if the little boy was a giant eggshell. "That's good. Even us confirmed bachelors need organization."

April looked over her shoulder. "How do you know the boys will be bachelors?"

He lifted one broad shoulder in dismissal. "Well, they're bachelors now."

"Just haven't met the right woman," she said with a smile.

He paused. "You're a big believer in marriage, are you, April?" He picked up the bag containing the boys' dinner and began to lead the way toward the kitchen.

"I want to get married if that's what you mean. I'm going to get married."

"Ah, the name change."

"Yes. Exactly."

"What will your name be then, Ms. Pruitt?"

She could feel herself growing warm. "I'm not completely sure yet, but I know it will happen. Technically, I'm not involved right now, but I believe it's possible to scientifically choose a mate and I've written a computer program to help me locate just the right man. It's only a matter of time." And telling him was only a matter of creating a barrier to her own foolish reactions to the darn, enticing man. No doubt he'd decided she was a looney after the statement she'd just made. Well, that was okay. Good, actually. Almost as good as things would be when she finally uploaded all the available data and located the man most suited to be a match for her. Then she would have a life's companion, a settled existence and none of the upheaval or distressing risks of a romantic entanglement. Her marriage would be a workable arrangement just as her parents' marriage had been.

Dylan took in her "wed by computer" speech, frowning slightly.

She raised her chin defensively.

"I see," he finally said with a slight nod. "Well, that's interesting. I wish you well on your search."

"Thank you," she said in a voice that sounded much too prim to her own ears. "I take it...that is, if you're a confirmed bachelor, then you don't approve of marriage?" she asked.

"I don't even think of marriage." As if he were afraid she might be thinking of putting him into her computer program. "Which is probably a good thing for the women of the world. I'd make a rotten husband."

She raised her brows. "Sounds as if some woman told you that."

He smiled. "Maybe one or two, but they were just stating the obvious."

She started to ask how he knew he'd be such a failure at marriage, but he must have seen the question coming.

"April?" His voice was gentle.

Instantly she forgot what she had been thinking.

"What?"

"I hate to change the subject, but I'm afraid I have a question. Something urgent."

She looked up at the sudden unrest in Dylan's eyes and wondered why, oh why, she had still not managed to get her heartbeat under control when she was trying so hard.

"I just need to know, do you have any idea how we get the food into these two?" He looked down at Jordie, and she realized that the little boy had placed his mouth on Dylan's arm and appeared to be chewing. Dylan's look of consternation grew, but he let the baby chew on.

She didn't have a clue what feeding a small child entailed, but attacking that problem seemed so much less daunting than thinking about how to calm her heartbeat when Dylan stared directly into her eyes. She searched frantically for an answer, since Jordie was obviously very much in need of something other than Dylan to chew on.

"I, well, I'm quite sure that we should feed them…systematically," she blurted out. After all, it was the way she tried to do everything. It was the only thing that had ever worked in her life. Keep things orderly and uncomplicated by anything illogical like lust or emotions.

"Okay then, April, we'll give it a whirl," Dylan whispered with a conspiratorial wink.

He said something else, too, but that wink spooked her so much that she didn't hear his next words. She was too busy running a list of Bernoulli numbers through her head. She wondered if Bernoulli had ever envisioned a woman using his equation to keep herself from thinking about what it would be like to lie in a man's arms in the night.

Well, that had been a bit of a disaster. Dylan studied the two little boys sitting in their food-spattered high chairs, then he looked down at his shirt which had once been white. He glanced over at April, who had bits of peaches in her pretty, tousled blond hair and across her cheek where she had raked her hand. A smear of peas lay like a banner across her right breast.

She should have looked completely worn and untouchable. Instead, Dylan found himself wanting to cup his hand over the stain on her breast, to thumb away the sticky mess.

Oh yeah, that would be incredibly smart. She was a woman looking for the perfect mate, a woman with deeply wounded eyes who was determined to hide those wounds from view. What she did not need in her life was a man who never intended to marry, offering her the opportunity to have her emotions battered again.

And what he didn't need was a woman who wanted a man who would stick around for the tough stuff.

"Looks like we lost the battle," he said, trying to tease his thoughts into a lighter vein.

April appraised his white shirt. "Well, the boys seem full, but I think you're going to have to burn that shirt or else frame it and call it art. I guess it's time for a bath, eh?"

For a second, his brain ceased functioning, and he thought April meant herself. Him. Together in a tub of warm water. Dylan was grateful that the edge of the table and a pair of black pants hid a multitude of sins, because it was going to take time or a lot of cold water before he recovered from that image.

Of course that wasn't what she meant at all. Somehow he managed to give a tight nod. "Another new experience. Who knew a man could learn so much at my age?"

But obviously he needed to learn even more. Like how to stop thinking of April Pruitt as a woman he'd like to see naked.

"Well, I always tell my students that a person is never too old to learn," April said. "Shall we get to it, then, Dylan?"

He nearly groaned, but instead he nodded tightly. Somehow during the next half hour, he managed not to drown Jordie in the soapy confines of a baby bathtub. He managed to mechanically swipe here and there and hang on to the chubby little boy's slippery skin, getting him at least a bit clean, while not doing something stupid like holding the child too close. No point making connections when this was just a three-week stint. It wouldn't be good for him, but it especially wouldn't be good for the boys. Dylan thought he was almost starting to get the hang of baby-bathing basics. Well, maybe not, he reconsidered, looking down into Jordie's less than happy face.

April was having an even rougher time of it, probably due to the fact that while Jordie at least sat quietly, clenching and unclenching his fists in the water as if trying to catch something, Sam was crowing and slamming his palms down flat against the surface. April was attempting to methodically work her way down the little boy's body with the washcloth, but Sam was a squirming little mass of baby. Dylan watched April take a long silent breath and hold it in.

"His head's well above the water," he said.

She nodded tightly, but she didn't speak. Her lips were a thin line of worry. He wondered what he'd gotten her into. He hadn't realized this would be so stressful for her.

"I think he's pretty clean now, anyway," he continued.

April studied Sam with a dubious expression. She breathed out, then in again and prepared to go on with her task.

"He'll do, April," Dylan said quietly. "Hey, it's your first day on the job. Cut yourself some slack."

"You're probably right. I can always try again another day," she said, in a voice that aimed at breezy but didn't quite fool Dylan. This lady had some serious issues with the baby thing. He wondered what they were, but that was none of his business. Whatever issues she had, she was going to err on the side of being too careful rather than too casual with the boys.

April lifted Sam from the water. When his wet little

body met hers while she struggled to wrap him in a towel, she went rigid for a second but quickly got herself under control.

And then the little boy looked up at her and gave her a glowing smile, peeking from beneath his towel.

For several long seconds April stared at Sam. And then she smiled back as if she couldn't do anything else. Something deep and warm turned within Dylan. It was as if a golden sunbeam had been released in his kitchen. The baby. The woman. A human link. Closeness.

And he felt something he'd experienced many times in his life. Cold. Tight. Caged with bars before his face.

Looking at the beauty of the woman and the child together was almost a spinning wheel of pain inside him.

He bent to Jordie and awkwardly bundled his little brother into a towel.

"Bed," he said firmly to the child who simply stared at him as if every word Dylan uttered was law.

"Buh," Jordie finally said.

"I'll take that as a yes," Dylan said.

"Seems to be a favorite word around here," April agreed.

And somehow, in spite of the fact that neither of them knew a thing about what they were doing, they managed to get the boys into decidedly loose and crooked diapers and into their pajamas. It only took the better part of an hour. At last the boys were placed into their cribs where they gazed at each other for long seconds before Sam laughed and waved and Jordie stared and waved back. After much cooing and changing positions, Dylan's croaking rendition of "House at Pooh Corner," April's hesitant reading of *If You Give a Mouse a Cookie,* some tears and lots of up and down stuff, both boys finally collapsed for the night.

Dylan was alone with April. They wandered out to the shadowed kitchen to clean up the water and the wet cloths.

He passed a bottle of baby shampoo to her, and their fingers slid against each other's. Automatically, his body reacted to her softness, to the slight gasp that slipped from her lips at the contact. He finally looked down at her, *really* looked at her.

The entire front of her white cotton blouse was damp from where the baby's wet body had rested against her, making it *revealing* white cotton. Clinging to skin that looked pale and fragile and oh so touchable.

He could see her pulse pounding in the delicate skin revealed by the vee of her blouse. The material looked cold against her skin, sticking to her, curving where she curved, and he suddenly wanted to release the tiny buttons that held the material closed, to peel back the cloth and reveal her glistening skin. He wanted to taste her lips, kiss his way down her throat, move lower to nuzzle breasts....

Dylan thought he saw April jerk slightly. He realized that he'd allowed his eyes to travel the path his thoughts had taken. He lifted his gaze and saw that her pretty violet eyes were wide and wary, and touched with an undeniable hint of desire as well.

She didn't look happy about the desire.

"Why don't you get some rest?" he suggested, leaning back and giving her some space. "It's been a day full of events you weren't expecting, and tomorrow promises to be just as busy. I'll clean up here."

That little chin came up. Those wary violet eyes turned to lavender steel. "You're paying me to help."

He smiled at her determination. "Believe me, you'll

help. Tomorrow. You think I can handle the two of them alone? You'll earn your keep, April. Don't worry.''

She stood silently, apparently trying to decide whether or not to allow him to win the battle. Finally she nodded. ''I'll see you in the morning,'' she agreed, and then she was gone.

He had made it. For long minutes, Dylan stood there just counting his blessings. He had gotten away without touching the woman. Maybe she needed some help, an extra hand, a part-time older woman who could aid her, who knew something about babies—and who would serve as a chaperone to keep him in line.

''What a great idea.'' He finished putting away the bathtubs and retreated to his room.

Hours later, he woke from sleep and thought he heard something. His first inclination was to leave it alone, but he had responsibilities now. He wasn't alone in the house tonight.

Throwing on a hunter-green robe, he moved into the hallway. No light in the boys' room or in April's room, either. That didn't seem right, he thought with a frown as he continued down the hall. Outside a small study, he paused. He pushed open the door that was half-ajar.

April rose from the desk where she had been seated at a small laptop computer. The ''Sam and Jordie's favorite things'' book that Vivian had left was lying open on the desk next to a C volume of the encyclopedia turned to an article on ''child psychology.''

''I'm sorry,'' she said with a small smile. ''I couldn't sleep, but just look what I've found. I've been reading and searching the Internet, and look at all the information there is on how to take care of toddlers.'' She pointed to a small, neat   stack   of   pages   she'd   printed   out.

"Feeding, bathing, potty-training," she said as if she'd just found the secret to long-lost pirate treasure on the Net.

"Potty-training, eh?" he asked with a pained smile.

"Well." She shook her head and blushed. "We probably don't need to go there. They're apparently too young, and I guess I just got carried away, but look…"

She picked up a small bound black notebook. "I've started journals for the boys. Information about their daily activities."

Her voice was laced with suppressed excitement. He flipped open the book and read. It was amazing how she'd managed to capture Jordie's personality in only a few sentences.

"Here's Sam's," she said, offering a blue journal. It was just as concise and revealing, and Dylan wondered how she could convey such warmth on paper when she was so nervous about getting too near the boys.

"What's that one?" he asked, gesturing to a blue and gold floral notebook.

She shook her head. "It's…nothing. Well, all right, it's mine," she admitted, when he raised one brow. "Just lists, mostly. You know, info about my marriage project."

Oh yes, her quest for the perfect man, the one she thought she'd found. Dylan felt something sharp and angry pass through him. He ignored it, unwilling to explore why he should care that April was narrowing in on her dream man. Most likely because he knew that "dream men" like his father had been could easily kill the dreams of vulnerable women.

But that wasn't his affair, and he didn't like the way he was embarrassing April.

"You're a talented writer," he said, gesturing to the boys' journals. "And I have to say that I'm relieved we're going to have some directions for tomorrow.'' He nodded toward her computer screen and the piles of information she'd discovered.

"Me, too," she said. "I love having everything laid out with clear, concise instructions. It's a weakness of mine. I practically shrieked with delight when I found this Web site on baby care." And she smiled and stretched dreamily the way a woman might after a night of wanton physical pleasure.

"It was good, was it?" Dylan asked, with a teasing smile.

"It was…exquisite," she whispered.

And he stepped closer, slowly, so that she could run if she needed to.

She didn't.

He bent to her, allowing her room to leave.

She stayed.

He slid his hands along the silk of her white dressing gown and pulled her toward him. He lowered himself to her, and his lips took hers. Slowly. Lightly. Pleasurably.

For ten seconds she was there with him, moving closer, touching him, moaning softly.

And then, with a small cry, she pulled back. Dylan looked down and saw confusion and then fear cloud those violet eyes. Obviously April was more than a woman who knew a lot about science and math and computers. She had a very passionate side she didn't want to acknowledge. But that fear… He'd seen a similar look in her eyes when Jason Olney had bid on her earlier today. And knowing that, there were no words, Dylan thought, that were harsh enough to explain how angry he was with himself. There was no excuse for what he'd just done.

Immediately he released her. He backed up several

steps. He picked up one of the journals and held it in front of him, so that she would know there was a barrier, however flimsy, between them, and that he didn't intend to touch her again.

"That was my mistake," he said carefully. "And I'm not even going to attempt to justify it or explain it. But I will tell you that now that I know I'm at risk of touching you, it won't happen again. I know how to control myself. You won't have to worry about me. Tomorrow I intend to hire some extra help for you, which I hope will make you feel a bit safer. For tonight, I suggest we both return to our rooms."

April nodded slowly. "All right, but..."

He waited.

"I apologize, too," she said. "I could have stopped you, but I didn't."

He nodded. "We both made mistakes, I suppose."

"I generally don't make them twice," she said, as if that would make him feel better. Somehow it didn't.

"A good practice," he agreed, and then he left her there, before he could let the night and the allure of her induce him to break his word after he'd just given it to her.

A long time later, he heard her door close. Good, she was safe in her room. He wouldn't follow her there. At least he hoped he wouldn't.

April lay awake, recalling the feel of Dylan's lips on her own and knew that she'd never be able to sleep. His touch had awakened something in her. Need. Desire. Unfulfilled passion. She was going to dream of those amber eyes of his tonight if she slept.

So who needed sleep, anyway?

What she needed was some way of getting Dylan out of her head.

Slowly, quietly, she climbed from her bed. No going back to the study this time. Instead, she propped her laptop on the nightstand. She called up her computer program and fiddled with it. She entered some more data, information about the kind of men who would be perfect for her. She had the program eliminate all the men with golden eyes, before she realized exactly what she was doing, but she didn't change it back. Then she asked the program to compute her new choices.

It chugged through the process, then the screen filled. There it was, three men, any one of which might be the perfect man for her. Greg Larraby, a professor, was the closest match. He was just right in so many ways. Similar backgrounds, similar interests, wasn't sure he wanted children.

She should contact him. His profile had come up before. She wondered why she hadn't gotten in touch with him yet.

Maybe she just hadn't had a good enough reason before. Now she did, and it was six foot three of beautiful man sleeping down the hall. A man with an incredible, gorgeous, muscled chest, she remembered, trying her best not to think about how it had felt to be held against that chest with those oh so talented lips on hers.

April closed her eyes, trying to block out the memory of being in Dylan's embrace, but all she succeeded in doing was making herself dizzy with desire.

"All right then," she finally whispered. "This calls for action. No holding back anymore."

And taking a sheet of paper from her supply, she forced herself to compose a letter. Breezy, cheerful, with lots of questions about Greg and a bit of information about herself. A very useful letter, since she couldn't write and think of Dylan at the same time.

Exhausted from her efforts and the hours without sleep, April finally fell into bed, sure that if she had dreams, they would be about a man of science, a man of mathematics, a practical man like Greg, her perfect mate.

But the first thought on her mind when she woke the next morning was a jolting one.

Heavens, but that man knew how to kiss. She wanted to feel those lips on hers right now.

And she knew the lips she had dreamed about, the man that had made love to her all night in restless fantasies, was in this house right now.

In a few minutes she would see him again. If she was lucky, she wouldn't take one look at him and recall those hazy fantasies that had made her sleep so pleasurable. Because the last thing she wanted to do was spend the next three weeks biting her tongue to keep herself from asking Dylan to touch her again.

Chapter Four

For a man who made his living making sure people's homes and businesses were safe from trespassers, he'd certainly done his share of trespassing yesterday, Dylan thought early the next morning.

"Do not go near April's mouth again, Valentine," he whispered, as he climbed from his shower, dried off and donned a crisp, white shirt. "From now on, you provide her with paid help and you concentrate on the things you've learned to do well. Like working with money and machines."

His words brought a sense of calm, some perspective. With casual ease, he picked up the first tie at hand, black like all his others, tied it with easy precision, and—lifting the telephone receiver—set out to find an agency that could provide a woman capable of training April in the skills a nanny would need. In less than no time, he had a candidate.

No doubt April would be pleased.

The thought brought a smile to his lips—and then a frown. Pleasing April wasn't on his list of things to do today.

April left her room a short time later armed with her sheets of instructions, the boys' journals and a strong determination to learn the ropes while not learning anything more about how Dylan's arms felt about her.

Not that she was going to have that opportunity. He was clearly no happier than she was that there was something physical arcing between them. She remembered that he had planned on hiring Agnes Mason and would have, too, if he hadn't been too busy rescuing her.

"So today you rescue him from baby-sitting so he can get back to work if he likes," she muttered to herself, marching down the hall to the boys' room.

Two little heads peeped over the tops of their cribs.

Sam even ventured a smile, and for a second April could see the vague resemblance to Dylan. No doubt about it, these little guys were going to follow in their brother's footsteps in the lady-killing department.

"You remember to treat the girls right when you start dating, sweetheart," she said to him, moving closer to Sam's crib so she could start the routine of dressing and feeding and figuring out just how tough this was going to be.

A low chuckle sounded behind her and she turned her head to see Dylan lounging in the doorway.

"You don't think they're ready for the dating scene yet, do you?"

A slow warmth began to climb up April's body. Thank goodness he couldn't know what had prompted her comment.

"It's never too early to learn how to treat a lady."

He raised one shoulder in a half shrug. "True, which

is why I've just employed a Mrs. McWerren to come in part-time this week and help you out a bit, as well as give both of us some coaching. I'm afraid I may have underestimated the amount of effort taking care of my brothers would be when I hired you. You must be feeling overwhelmed.''

What April was feeling was nervous. She was in the middle of the room, between two of the most adorable babies she'd ever seen and one of the most achingly seductive men she'd ever met. Temptation lay all around her, and she wanted to close her eyes, click her heels three times and disappear.

She took a deep breath. ''I think I've got things under control.'' So why was she crushing the pages she held in her arms? Quickly, she loosened her grip. ''But I thank you for the offer.''

''I'm not accusing you of being incapable, April. I'm just saying that I may have been a bit shortsighted.''

''This Mrs. McWerren—wouldn't you be better off having her take care of the boys?'' April couldn't help glancing over at Jordie, who was rubbing his eyes with chubby little fists. No question about it, the best thing for all concerned would be if she got out of here fast.

Dylan shook his head. ''She can only spare a few hours each day. I need someone all day and night.''

His voice rasped over the last few words. April swallowed hard at the thought of Dylan all night.

''I—I didn't mean that I didn't want the job. The boys are adorable and you're giving a great deal of money to Safe House. I should be grateful for the opportunity.''

That line about gratitude was exactly what her mother would have said, but in a much sterner voice. And she would have been right, too, April thought. It was darn foolish to let her emotions start getting in the way of making sane decisions. She'd learned that some time ago.

She squared her shoulders and looked up to find Dylan studying her. "You don't have to be grateful," he said, his voice a near whisper. "I didn't hire you for any altruistic reasons. I was…"

She knew what he had been going to say, but she also knew that he was too much a gentleman to say it. That thought alone made April smile. "You were desperate," she offered.

He opened his mouth to do the polite thing and protest, but she held up her hand. "No, we both know that neither one of us has a clue how to go on. The poor boys are at our mercy."

Dylan chuckled, and the sound wrapped itself around her in such a seductive way that she almost wished she was the kind of woman who could make a man laugh often.

"But I suppose," she said, rushing to block those thoughts, "most new parents don't know any more than we do." She hadn't when she'd been pregnant. And she'd had friends who had told her horror stories of the first few months of parenting.

Their words had sent bitter longing and pain through her, and she'd wanted to scream for them to stop, but then she remembered that they didn't know her past. No one but her mother knew, her mother who had always been full of sound advice about following her head, not her heart. Even now she could almost hear Marlene Pruitt admonishing her daughter not to be a fool like her grandmother had been. And imagining her mother lecturing her was almost as good as having the flesh-and-blood woman right here instead of in St. Louis where she now lived.

April squared her shoulders. "I think we'll be just fine, Dylan. All we need is a little organization and determination and the right guides," she said, holding up her instruction sheets. "I'll just finish reading these."

But at that moment, Sam fell and hit his chin. He set up a tremendous wailing and Jordie's eyes grew big and scared. He started to cry, fat tears wending their way down his cheeks.

April stared down at the sheets in her hands, hoping desperately for a miracle. Maybe the right instruction sheet would fall out, or Mrs. McWerren would show up right now.

Jordie looked as if his little heart was breaking right before her eyes.

She cast distressed eyes Dylan's way and found that he was looking a bit pale for such a big man. He nodded at her. She set down the papers. Together they stepped forward. Dylan picked up Sam, April picked up Jordie. The warm little body fit against hers too easily, the damp little cheek touched her own. She wanted to cry, too.

Dylan was awkwardly patting Sam's back. "No need to cry."

Whether it was the sound of that low, deep voice at such close quarters, the knowledge that he was being held quite safely by a very large male, or something else, Sam suddenly looked up at his brother, and the wailing stopped dead.

Jordie turned to his brother, his own snuffling fading out, his breathing still uneven.

Dylan's eyes met April's over the babies' heads. "That was tense," he whispered.

She'd never realized that the sight of a man holding a baby could be very sexy, but there was no denying the fact that Dylan cradling his little brother was even more devastating than Dylan just standing there looking gorgeous in the usual sense.

There was also no denying that Jordie's little fingers were clutching her shirt tightly. As if she were his lifeline—or his mother.

No fair, her heart cried on both counts.

"So…" Dylan said, clearing his throat, his golden gaze holding her own, "how would you say that we did that? Do you think the technique could be replicated?"

April dragged her gaze away from his to look at Sam, who was sucking on his thumb and looking utterly content. She couldn't help smiling at the beatific expression on the little boy's face or the skeptical note in Dylan's voice.

"I guess I'd say that Sam just likes his big brother," she said softly.

A slightly horrified look crossed Dylan's face. "Hmm, most likely beginner's luck."

She grinned. "Could be that, too." And she disentangled herself from Jordie's grip, smoothing his hair from his face as she placed him in his playpen with his favorite stuffed playmates.

He whimpered slightly and April's breath caught in her throat, but before she could follow her instincts and catch him back up in her arms, he made his way to a busy box with lots of buttons and wheels and was instantly lost in play.

"Fickle like all men," she said with a smile.

But when she turned, Dylan had placed Sam in the playpen, too, and her tempting employer was studying her with interest.

"Fickle like all men?" he asked.

"Just an expression," she said hastily.

But Dylan didn't nod or laugh. "You were probably

right the first time," he said, his voice low and deep and incredibly sexy, incredibly close. "Most men are fickle."

"But not you," she said, expecting him to say that. Wasn't that what most men would do, try to convince the woman that they were the exception?

"Especially me," he whispered. "Better put that on your list for your perfect mate, April. Find a man who's reliable and steady. I guarantee that his last name won't be Valentine."

And he left the room, the silence closing in behind him, broken only by the cooing and gurgles of the babies.

April peered down the hall as he moved away, his back long and strong, his stride decisive. He walked quickly, as if he couldn't wait to get away from her or the boys.

She couldn't help her thoughts, and before she knew it she was opening her mouth.

"I know you have work, but will you stay until your Mrs. McWerren arrives?" she called.

He turned, his golden gaze meeting her own. She did her best to hide her nervousness and her fear at being left alone with the little boys. In fact, she didn't know what was more frightening to her, being alone with the babies or with Dylan. Both posed their own kinds of risks. She had the feeling that the risks surrounding the man were greater and longer lasting, but at least she wasn't worried about hurting him the way she was with Jordie and Sam. Her own safety and peace of mind would have to be set aside today.

The lives of babies were at stake.

The feelings and fears of one woman didn't count for

much against that. She would risk Dylan, if he would stay.

"Dylan?"

He smiled then, and her breath did some strange whooshing thing in her throat.

"I wasn't leaving, April. I was just going to answer the door. I just heard a car pull up in the drive. I'm guessing that help has arrived."

Help. She certainly could use some of that.

"That's good," she said, breathing out a great sigh of relief. Of course, now that Mrs. McWerren had arrived, Dylan wouldn't need to stay. She'd probably see very little of him in the next few weeks.

Except at night when Mrs. McWerren had gone home and she and Dylan were more or less alone and free to make mistakes.

How many days had Vivian said she'd be gone? Dylan thought when he left to go open the door. Almost three weeks? Too long. But maybe he could already mark off one day. If he knew Viv, she'd counted yesterday and every minute of the time away from her children.

For his own part, he was counting the seconds until April Pruitt would be walking out of his life.

Was there ever a woman with eyes that revealed so much of her soul? She'd been crushed when Jordie had sobbed in her arms.

And when *he* had gazed down at her, he could almost swear she'd held her breath. She'd probably remembered that he'd touched her without even being invited. Or else she'd remembered that he was not the kind of man she wanted.

Which was a damned good thing, since he didn't want *any* kind of woman, least of all a vulnerable one.

"Hiring this one was a mistake, Valentine," he muttered, as he moved toward the door and willed another day of the calendar to melt away quickly. "She's a temptation, and she's at risk, both from you and from the boys, too, for some reason. She has secrets, and she has dreams of marrying some perfect guy."

So, maybe he should help her, with the boys and with her dreams as well. What was wrong with encouraging April to pursue the man she was really looking for?

Nothing, except that he had the strongest urge to bend her back over his arm and kiss the delicate hammering pulse at her throat. He wanted to do more, too, but he wouldn't allow himself to go there, not even in his thoughts.

If he did, Mrs. McWerren was going to be very shocked when she opened the door and found a fully aroused male standing in the entrance.

Chapter Five

"Oh, you make such a lovely, lovely couple. And your children are sooo beautiful. You must be very proud."

Mrs. McWerren had followed Dylan into the blue-and-white parlor where he and April had decided the boys could play. The plump lady with the well-scrubbed face was beaming at April.

"May I hold one of the babies, Mrs. Valentine?" she asked.

"Yes, of course. This is Sam," April said, slipping him into Mrs. McWerren's outstretched arms, "but I'm not...that is, Mr. Valentine and I aren't...we certainly don't and haven't ever—"

She thought she heard Dylan choking behind her, but when she turned, he simply smiled that lazy, sexy smile and placed a soothing hand on the small of her back. His touch warmed her skin all the way through her clothing, and she was anything but soothed. The urge to step closer to him, to breathe in the scent of his aftershave lotion and his skin was unnerving and maddening. She took a deep breath to calm herself, but that only sent his fingertips sliding over her body.

Think about Greg Larraby, April ordered herself, but all she could register was the strength in Dylan's fingers. A choked sound slipped from between her lips.

"Shh," Dylan said, leaning close to her as Mrs. McWerren talked to the baby.

"She thinks we're married," April whispered. And being married to Dylan meant that she would be sleeping with him. It brought forth visions she could barely handle without squirming. The thought that other people might be thinking the same thing was distressing. Especially since she would never experience the pleasure of Dylan's body filling her own.

April desperately hoped she wasn't blushing. She couldn't tell, because her every nerve was centered on Dylan's touch. And then, when he pulled away, her body seemed to know that it had missed out on something delicious. She fought to stand still as Dylan moved toward his newest employee.

"Mrs. McWerren, I'm afraid I must apologize." Dylan's voice was so commanding that the lady looked up from her game of pat-a-cake with Sam. "April and I aren't husband and wife."

The plump little woman's eyes grew round, but then she simply shrugged. "Oh, there's a lot of that going around."

Dylan chuckled, and April caught her breath. "There's nothing going on around here," she said quickly, but she didn't miss the look on Dylan's face. All right, so there *was* something going on. The air practically reeked of estrogen and testosterone every time Dylan glanced her way. Still...

"Mr. Valentine does not—we're not—well, heavens, I'm just the baby-sitter."

Mrs. McWerren looked puzzled then. "I thought *I* was the baby-sitter. And these aren't your children? The agency said…well, I guess they just said that you had two babies." She looked to Dylan for clarification.

He shrugged. "I have two babies. My brothers," he said simply. "But Ms. Pruitt has agreed to help me watch them for the next few weeks. I have my reasons for hiring her. Unfortunately, neither of us knows that much about babies."

Mrs. McWerren frowned, clearly confused. April wouldn't have blamed the woman if she questioned Dylan's sanity. He'd hired a baby-sitter who knew nothing about babies, and now he was hiring another baby-sitter while the first was still present.

"Mr. Valentine very generously offered money to a local charity at a job auction and he somehow ended up with me, a baby-sitter with no experience when he clearly needs someone who knows something about young children," she explained. "We understand that you are available for limited periods of time, and we really need an instructor."

Tilting her head, Mrs. McWerren looked at Sam as if to ask him if he was associated with these two silly people. She marched over to the other playpen and took out Jordie, who settled into her arms with no problem.

"You need someone to teach you how to take care of these little dears?" she asked.

"They're my baby brothers, my only immediate relatives," Dylan explained. "We want to give them the best care possible. We would appreciate it if you'd share your expertise."

Mrs. McWerren looked as if Dylan had just taken her

into his arms and kissed her silly. "Well, of course I'd be delighted to teach you what I know," she said, beaming at the two of them. "You'll be surprised at how easy this is."

April looked at Dylan and the babies and knew that there would be absolutely nothing easy about this, not with this man, and not for a woman with April's history with men and babies.

"Well, we're ready then," Dylan said softly, and against her will, the sound of his voice drew April in. Reality finally hit. For the next few weeks, she was going to live with that voice, that body, that sexy smile. She was going to be in a constant state of desire.

But, she promised she was *not* going to allow herself to fall prey to those emotions. She would not be her grandmother, nor would she repeat the mistakes she'd already made. If it killed her, she was going to ignore those overwhelming emotions she felt every time Dylan was near.

Weakly, she smiled at Mrs. McWerren and swallowed hard.

"I'm ready," she agreed.

But ready for what? she wondered.

All right, this was getting out of hand, Dylan thought, as Mrs. McWerren demonstrated the basics of changing a diaper and thrust Sam into his arms. Dylan took the baby, trying not to note that the little boy was smiling, snuggly and baby-scented. He held him carefully, but resisted the urge to pull him closer. No point in getting too involved when Sam would be gone shortly. It was a routine Dylan had learned long ago. Don't form attachments, don't notice the details of other people too much.

But that was exactly the problem, because for some

reason he was noticing everything about April. While Dylan kept an eye on Sam as he set him down and attempted to replicate the steps Mrs. McWerren had taken to diaper the baby, April was alternately babbling softly to Jordie, then, as if catching herself doing something wrong, turning all businesslike and quiet, her violet eyes sad. She was obviously drawn to the baby and yet extremely uncomfortable. As he'd noted before, something wasn't right.

And since he was the one who had put her in this position, what else could he do but attempt to take her mind off whatever was bothering her?

"Whoa, Sam, you're making me look bad, aren't you, kid?" he asked, eyeing his little brother, who was squirming around. "Look at April and Jordie. She's already got the diaper on him, and it's actually straight. Help me out here, won't you?"

Sam might not have understood exactly what Dylan was saying, but he responded to his big brother's teasing tone, wrinkling his nose and giggling as he waved his feet around in the air. When Dylan bent over him to fasten the first of the two diaper tabs, glancing at April out of the corner of his eye, Sam grabbed a handful of his hair and pulled.

"Sam, have I told you that you're a little devil today?" he teased, and he disentangled himself, flipping the two tabs closed as he looked up at April in triumph.

"Not bad, eh?" he asked.

She smiled at him. "It's very nice, Dylan, except you appear to have the diaper on backward."

He knew that. Sam appeared to know it, too, since he was laughing, but it was worth it just to see the relaxed, amused expression in April's eyes.

Dylan shrugged. "Let's show her we can do this, little

bud,'' he suggested, quickly pulling the tabs loose, tossing a new diaper beneath Sam and closing it the right way.

"You're fast," April said, feigning admiration. "Give him a pat on the back, Mrs. McWerren."

The lady chuckled. "I think he's probably a bit too full of himself as it is. Some men don't need encouraging."

A slight pink flush spread over April's fair skin. Oh, but it would be nice to be encouraged by April, Dylan couldn't help thinking. Nice, but wrong.

"Ah, Mrs. McWerren, you're breaking my heart," he teased. "Not even one kind word about my diaper-changing skills?"

"Hmmph, I'm thinking that you probably have a lot of practice removing clothes and putting them back. On women at least," she admonished. "A diaper wouldn't be any real challenge for you, but just wait until one of these sweethearts starts to wail and refuses to stop. What will you do then?"

Dylan looked down at Sam, who was still giggling. He glanced at Jordie who, while not laughing, was smiling angelically up at April

Of course, he knew that they would cry. Didn't all babies do that? And he didn't have a clue what to do when and if that should happen. The very thought made him feel as if a bubble of fear was growing inside him. But he was pretty sure that April would be more than afraid. She would be brokenhearted if one of the boys started to cry and she couldn't figure out how to help.

Dropping to his knees before Mrs. McWerren, Dylan winked slowly at the lady. "Mrs. McWerren, I beg you, tell us the secret of how to dry a baby's tears."

Both babies' eyes grew round.

April covered her mouth with her hand, then shook her head. "You're terrible, Dylan. Mrs. McWerren will think that you aren't taking baby-sitting seriously."

"Mrs. McWerren is thinking that this one is a dangerous flirt. If you're smart, you'll watch yourself, April," the woman answered.

Dylan couldn't help it. He turned to see April's reactions to Mrs. McWerren's words. It bothered him to see the distress in April's eyes.

"She's safe with me," he said solemnly, quietly. "That's a promise, and I take promises very seriously, Mrs. McWerren."

The rosy-cheeked little woman looked from Dylan to April and back again. "I believe you do, Dylan," she finally said. "Now if you want to know my methods for distracting a baby from crying, you'll get up off your knees and listen."

He did. For the next hour, Mrs. McWerren talked. The boys grew sleepy and were put down for naps, and she talked some more. April was taking furious notes on a laptop computer, tapping away as if her teacher's words were pure gold.

Dylan simply listened.

Eventually, the phone rang. It was his office calling, which initiated a conversation about his business.

"If you make peoples' houses secure, you should see to securing your own a bit better," Mrs. McWerren said. "Babies need special consideration when it comes to safety."

"I'm discovering that," he agreed, looking at Sam.

"Would your business be able to help us?" April asked. "I thought Valentine Enterprises dealt more with protecting homes from burglars and that kind of thing." She turned those bright, inquisitive eyes on him.

"It does," he agreed, "as well as protection from fires and things like that, but we also get involved in more specialized areas. I always have people out combing the fields for the latest technology to make every home safer for the occupants. Babies would be a special field. Maybe we should go over to the office to see what choices we have."

"You want *me* to go with you?"

He supposed she was right. Mrs. McWerren would know more about what was needed, but the lady was shaking her head. "Offices scare me. Babies don't. You two go find something to make this house safe for the babies. I'll watch them."

So Dylan soon found himself driving April to Valentine Enterprises' home office. For the first time in a long time, he realized that he was nervous about having a woman beside him. Maybe it was because his business was such a part of him.

"Is Valentine Enterprises a family business?"

"If you mean, did I inherit it from my father, no. I was always interested in electronic gadgets." Machines had always been easy. They never failed a person, at least under normal circumstances, and they gave exactly what one expected of them. Besides, Dylan had always wanted something that was strictly his own. Since he'd started the business, he'd had that, and it was all he needed.

April chuckled. "That must be why you have so many buttons on your dashboard."

"And you want to know what they are, don't you?" He couldn't keep the smile from his voice.

"Of course I do. Who wouldn't?" She folded her hands in her lap, waiting, and for a moment Dylan couldn't help wondering what it would be like to lie with his head in her lap. She'd be soft, he bet. He could turn his head and kiss her skin through the silk of her dress.

Automatically he frowned, mentally chastising himself.

She blinked. "Perhaps I shouldn't have asked," she said softly. "I know I tend to be a bit nosy when I run across something hi-tech. A failing of mine."

He shook his head. "Not a failing. You're a teacher, a woman of science. You're supposed to be curious about new things. Unfortunately, there's nothing here that you probably haven't seen. A GPS, a hot button link to my office, a weather-sensor control for the wipers and defroster."

"You like gadgets, don't you?" she asked, even though his tone had been very casual.

"I like the sense of control they give me."

He turned to glance her way, and she was studying him carefully. Finally she nodded. "It's a good thing that you have your own company then, if you like to be in control."

"It helps," he said with a shrug. But he was pretty sure that April already knew a lot about the rush that being in control gave a person. Wasn't she the woman who was going to choose a husband with a computer program? The very thought of some man staring at her picture on a computer screen made him edgy. He wasn't sure why, but he was reasonably certain that he shouldn't dig any deeper into this area. She had the right to make her own choices.

"Come on, let me show you around," he said. Dylan parked the car and escorted April inside.

April's eyes lit up as soon as they walked through the doors of Valentine Enterprises. The lobby was decorated in deep green, pale gold and oak with a myriad of plants and fountains scattered throughout. A combination of skylights and lacy fixtures teamed up to create an illusion of sunlight in dappled patterns, like light filtering into a forest. The reception desk was caught in a beam of fairy-like light, and the dark green walls of the room sparkled slightly, like the gleam of sunlight on water, tempting a person to touch. "You've done such clever things with the lighting and the fountains…and oh my, the music," she said, as she ran her hand across a marble wall and a trill of music played. "How do you do that?" she asked, nearly jumping back, her eyes big with delight.

He couldn't help enjoying the way those eyes lit up, at how she struggled to maintain an air of dignity when she was clearly as enchanted as either Jordie or Sam would be if they touched something and it played music.

"And what does this have to do with security systems?" she asked.

"Security's our bread and butter, but I like to give my employees the freedom to explore other areas as well. And customers who are enthusiastic about the latest security systems also tend to get excited about other technological inventions. Go touch that one," he suggested, and she wandered off to another wall. The song that emanated from her fingertips was "House at Pooh Corner," the song Dylan had sung to Jordie and Sam the night before.

"Dylan," she drawled. "Are you psychic?"

No, but he almost wished that he were. He would love to know the mysteries behind April Pruitt, even if he wasn't prepared to ask. Asking implied interest, and interest in a woman like this implied things that couldn't be.

"I'm just good with a telephone," he said. "The music is programmable. When I knew that you were coming with me, I sent someone at the office on a search for the right tune."

"That was thoughtful."

He shook his head. "It was selfish. You've been looking rather nervous all day. You have a nice smile. I wanted to see it and to give you a bit of a breather."

"That's why you suggested I come with you while Mrs. McWerren watched the boys. But Dylan, taking care of the boys is my job. It's why you hired me."

He ran his fingers over the wall. "Well, Mrs. McWerren was dying for a moment alone with the twins, wasn't she? Besides, you worked hard today and will again. This trip isn't purely recreational for that matter."

And he led her through a large set of mahogany doors into a room full of noise and people and gadgets. When he and April came through the door, many people smiled and waved, but one man came forward, a big smile on his face.

"Jenner," Dylan said, returning a smile. "Have you got everything ready? This is Ms. Pruitt, and I warn you, she knows her computers."

"Then maybe we'll have to go low-tech to impress her, Dylan." He took April's hand in his own. "I'm pleased to meet another technology fan," he said. "Now the two of you are interested in babies?"

Dylan had to fight off the thought of doing anything with April that would result in a baby, but she was blushing and that only made him want to see what happened to the blush where it dipped beneath the vee of her white blouse.

"Um, maybe we should begin with the newest baby monitors," he suggested to Jenner.

"Oh, yes," April agreed. "We need to keep an eye on things."

"If Dylan's brothers are anything like him, I'm sure that's true," Jenner said. "The man's into everything. In fact, he's far better equipped to show you around than I am. I'll just show you where I've set everything up that you asked for."

Several minutes later, Dylan and April walked around a huge room filled with television monitoring systems, audio monitoring systems, tools that would enable a person to erect an invisible playpen that would chime if a child crossed the perimeters, sensors that could detect a child falling into a swimming pool and air purifiers to protect young lungs as well as the usual manual door locks, cabinet locks, corner protectors and covers for electric outlets.

"You're very thorough, aren't you?" she asked teasingly. "Dylan, where on earth did you come up with all this stuff?"

"I didn't invent any of it," he said, holding his hands out.

"No, but you gathered all the material, and this is only one aspect of your business, didn't you say? It's amazing."

"Security is very important to people. I want them to find what they're looking for. It makes me feel good to be able to provide that sense of safety, of being cared for. Especially to children."

April glanced up at his tone. She gazed into those golden eyes of his. This was a man who had implied that his father wasn't domestic, that he didn't like children or want them, and yet Dylan clearly felt some responsibility for the children of the world. She saw it in the way he protected his brothers, even though he did his best to maintain an emotional distance. She couldn't help wondering what had happened in his childhood to foster his concern for the little ones of the world.

It really wasn't any of her business, was it? She should keep her questions to herself, but…

"If your father always left when things got too domestic, does that mean that you didn't have much security as a child?"

Dylan leveled those awesome eyes on her. "Uh-oh, I'm afraid I've stirred up the concerned schoolteacher in you, but there's no need for concern. As you can see," he said, gesturing with his hand, "I've done extremely well."

His eyes darkened, and she knew that no matter where he'd ended up, his childhood had been less than ideal. Her question had obviously brought back unpleasant memories he didn't care to tap into. She'd trespassed on his privacy.

Unable to stop herself, she placed her small hand over his larger one. "I'm sorry for asking. Sometimes I'm just too nosy."

"And sometimes I'm too reticent. You're living in my house, April. You're caring for my brothers. You need to know something of their background and I can tell you that. Don't worry too much about Sam and Jordie. Like me, they had a father who was never there, but Viv isn't anything like my mother. My mother spent her whole life trying to win my father back. She felt, justifiably so, I suppose, that I was a deficit in that game, and so she tended to farm me out to her relatives who only agreed to take me in because she paid them well for the job of raising me. I was passed around a lot, but that won't be happening to Jordie and Sam. You can see that Viv loves them."

Just as it was clear that neither of his parents had loved Dylan, April thought. It struck her that her own mother had been harsh at times, but that had been born of worry and caring, and it had been justified. What must it be like not to have anyone to care at all, to be shoved from one house to the next, unwanted and alone? All the riches in the world couldn't make up for that kind of pain.

But Dylan was shaking his head.

"Don't waste your time worrying about something that happened long ago and is long buried, April. I didn't tell you that to elicit your sympathy, but to show you why I went into this business. People crave security, they need it, and I like making them feel that their homes are havens that can't be breached. As for me, I learned what I wanted early on, and I went after it. Believe me, I have everything I want or need."

And he'd already told her that he didn't want or need a wife. Well, so what? Not everyone needed a mate. Some people preferred the company of thousands to the company of one. Dylan must be such a man. And who could deny that he could have as much company as he wanted whenever he wanted?

He gave pleasure to many women and moved on. Which meant that he was the very kind of man she was running from.

But those beautiful, deep amber eyes made her suddenly wish that she could be the kind of woman who could make love with a man for just one night and never need any more.

Chapter Six

April sat in the grass on Dylan's front lawn and tried not to think about the fact that Dylan was inside installing all the goodies they'd brought home yesterday to make the house safe for Sam and Jordie. It was such a domestic thing to do for a man who spurned domesticity. Somehow that made it very sensual.

Where had that word come from? Nowhere good. She quickly turned her attention back to Jordie and Sam, who were playing with grapefruit-size rubber balls. Or something *like* playing. Sam seemed to be trying to eat his, and Jordie was sitting on his and then falling off again, giggling softly.

She smiled at their sweet if futile antics.

Even she knew better than to try to get the two boys to roll the ball to each other. According to everything that she'd read about eighteen-month-olds, they just weren't ready for group play, but they were a delight to watch just as they were.

"Baw," Sam said, holding his toy up, apparently so that she could take a bite of the already wet rubber.

Instead she ducked her head and kissed his fat little hand, delighting him into a gurgly smile, but when she raised her head, something felt very wrong, as if something was out of place or the world was off-balance. The feeling had nothing to do with Sam, who was still gloriously happy, and it wasn't anything amiss with Jordie, who was now lying on the ball without any more success than he'd had sitting on it.

No, it was just a sensation. Creepy, like an old house at midnight when the lights were on and the world could see in but those inside couldn't see out into the blackness. Like eyes on her back. April raised her chin and looked around.

She felt as if she were being watched, but Mrs. McWerren wouldn't be here until later today, and Dylan was still inside.

Besides, it wasn't Dylan, anyway. When Dylan was around, she felt no menace. The sensations he called forth in her were tantalizingly warm, fluid, sometimes hot.

This was cold.

And suddenly April realized that Sam was shoving the ball up into her face. Repeatedly. The wet, cold ball. That was all it was. She shook her head and smiled up at him, happy to know she'd just been imagining things.

Still, she scooped up the babies and bundled them inside.

And as she neared the house and moved closer to Dylan, a small thrill shot through her. A sense of anticipation, of longing. But that was just plain wrong. No doubt about it. More husband-hunting was in order. Tonight she would refine her program and add more data to ensure a perfect match.

That would certainly be better than thinking about Dylan sleeping just a few doors away.

She wondered what he slept in. Probably nothing.

That was her last thought as she rounded the corner and came upon Dylan sitting on the floor. He wore a white shirt and jeans that molded to his thighs. There was a tool belt around his waist, a screwdriver in his hand and a smile on his lips.

"April, why are you blushing?" he asked. "Have these boys been misbehaving?"

Not the boys. Just her imagination.

"These boys are absolute angels," she told him. "Any mother would love them for her own."

But she was reminded that his mother hadn't loved him. She remembered with a sudden ache that she had once had the chance to be a mother and had lost it through her own misadventures. She looked at Dylan with eyes loaded with regret.

He studied her carefully. "I think I've finished here," he said gently, quietly, slowly. "Let's play."

And her mind short-circuited.

Why had he put it that way? Dylan thought, the moment the words left his mouth. Associating April with play was dangerous, and well he knew it. But he'd been fooling with the security system all morning, Mrs. McWerren wasn't around, and April had been left to manage with the boys alone. It just hadn't seemed fair. She needed a respite of some type.

"What—what should we play?" she asked.

Instantly a vision of April in his bed, clad in a scrap

of white lace and nothing else chased away any other thoughts Dylan had been having.

He sucked in a deep breath.

"Let's visit the garden," he suggested. "Then I thought we might take the boys for a walk. There's a playground only a block or two away."

Was that a sigh of relief she let out? A sharp pain shot through Dylan. An unfamiliar pain. He wasn't used to women backing away from his attentions.

But maybe he should get used to it, he thought. She clearly was behaving with more common sense than he was.

"That sounds perfect," she finally said. "Would you like a baby?" and she offered Jordie up to his big brother.

"I believe I will," he said, grinning back, even though he was a bit nervous at the prospect of Jordie. This little brother was more insecure than Sam. He needed more, and Dylan knew he didn't have too much to give beyond teasing and tickles.

But he led his little pretend family out into the garden. He watched as April carefully took Sam's hand and then Jordie's when Dylan set him down. She slowly led their tottering steps down the path, peering over her shoulder at Dylan now and then.

"We have to walk slowly so Dylan can keep up," she told the boys with a big smile.

They looked back at him, almost as if they understood. Dylan *did* understand. He'd been walking too quickly, almost tripping up on the feet of the little boys, though he hadn't noticed until he was almost on top of them, so intent was he on studying the interactions of the three of them.

"Slowly, my lovely baby-sitter," he agreed.

She nodded and moved ahead, her hips gently swaying as she led the boys. Suddenly Sam stopped and turned. He pointed, his little lips curving into an *O*. He started jabbering as he focused on a patch of bright yellow marigolds.

"Yes, Sam, that's a *Calendula Officinalis,* otherwise known as a marigold," April said, "and those red-and-white ones are *Dianthus barbatus,* also called Sweet William."

Dylan raised a brow at April's use of the more formal terms, but she'd apparently already noticed the slipup herself.

"Some of my students last year were taking Latin. We got in the habit of sharing with the rest of the class. I suppose Jordie and Sam don't need that much information. I'm still not quite used to the junior set."

"But you're good with them. They obviously feel comfortable," he pointed out. "Must be that maternal tone."

Her eyes darkened at that and for a moment her smile vanished. Then as if she were afraid that he would see a part of her she didn't want to share, she took a visible breath and straightened.

"I believe you made promises about a playground? Are you going to go through with that?"

"You think I was lying?"

"You don't look like a man who frequents playgrounds."

She was right. "April, you're breaking my heart."

She smiled at that, then glanced down at the boys. "Don't pay any attention to him. It is, technically speaking, not possible to break a heart."

Dylan laughed. "Okay, I am, technically, incorrect,

but I promised a playground and I intend to produce a playground. Anyone want to swing?''

"Swing," Jordie said. "Me swing." It was a long speech for the normally quiet little boy.

"You heard the man," Dylan said to April. "To the swings."

And he held out one arm as if he were escorting a debutante to a ball rather than leading his cute little brothers and their prettier-than-spring-flowers baby-sitter off to the swings and slides.

The park was just as he'd said, a mere two blocks away, but it was still too far for the boys to walk, and they hadn't taken the stroller, so by the time they got there, Dylan had babies in his arms and April by his side.

The boys' eyes lit up when the swings came in sight. Obviously, Viv took them to playgrounds now and again. Sam was practically jumping up and down in Dylan's arms, and April quickly reached to take him so that Dylan wouldn't drop Jordie.

"Let's go try them out, sweetie, okay?" she said, and Sam gave her a most adoring smile, the smile of a child whose every wish in life has been granted and who was clearly, utterly besotted with the woman taking care of him.

Dylan envied his little brother the freedom to be so candid about his wants and needs and reactions.

And for the first time since he'd first seen April with the boys, she forgot to look worried. The smile she gave Sam was one of pure pleasure and adoration. She absolutely glowed, and Dylan felt as if he'd been hit with a cannonball. For half a second, he felt sorry for Jason Olney and his futile attempts to get the lady to go out with him.

But only for a second. He was too busy watching April to spare any thoughts for the man from her past.

"Let me help," he said gently, slipping Jordie into a swing and fastening him in, then taking Sam from April and lifting him into the baby swing while she made sure he was secure. Together they stood, gently pushing the happy little boys alongside the parents and nannies who filled the park.

"Looks like you two have your hands full," one elderly woman said.

"Oh, they're no trouble," April said, and Dylan smiled. She'd apparently already forgotten that Jordie and Sam had once again ended up with oatmeal in their hair this morning, and Jordie had shed big, heartbreaking tears when Sam had accidentally sat on his fingers.

For long minutes they pushed the boys in the swings, the little feet dangling, the sound of laughter filling the air.

"You have such pretty children," another woman said, cutting into Dylan's thoughts, "but then why not? You have such a pretty wife."

Immediately April looked wary again. She was on the verge of trying to explain their situation again, when Dylan grinned at her and shook his head.

She grinned back and wrinkled her nose.

"Why thank you," she said instead. "I do like to think the boys look like me."

The woman stared down at the little boys. "Why, they do look a lot like you."

Dylan let out a long sigh. "I only wish they had a bit of my coloring or...something. It's awfully embarrassing when people think my wife and the mailman resemble my sons more than I do."

"Yes, the mailman *does* have beautiful blue eyes," April agreed, with a dreamy soft sound to her voice.

Dylan raised one brow, but she was looking completely innocent. The poor woman was backing away toward her own charges, frowning at April and shaking her head.

"Oh, I shouldn't have said that," April whispered when she had gone. "At least not that last bit. It was...well, I think it was mean and not like me at all. I hate lying. But the part about us being married, I guess...that is, it just seems too complicated to keep explaining our real situation."

"Yes, I know what you mean," Dylan said. "Does the mailman really have beautiful eyes?"

She blinked wide then and laughed when he smiled at her. "Yours are much nicer," she told him consolingly.

He shouldn't have felt good about that, but he did.

"Oh, no," she suddenly said. "Dylan, look."

He looked down and saw that both of the boys had fallen asleep, their little heads leaning at awkward angles as they slumped over the sides of the yellow plastic baby swings.

"Oh, no, I wasn't even paying attention. What if something had happened to them?" April's eyes were huge and worried and generously laden with guilt.

"They're just sleeping, April," he said gently. "No reason to worry."

"But I wasn't watching them."

"They were fully strapped in. We were right here. There's no reason for you to chastise yourself just because they fell asleep without your knowledge while you were talking."

But he knew that her guilt lay partly in the fact that

they hadn't just been talking. They had been flirting. He felt a stab of guilt himself. Flirting with April could only lead down dead-end roads.

He dropped the subject as April lifted the boys out of the swings and gave them to him. In silence they returned to the house where Mrs. McWerren had already arrived for a short afternoon session. Together they trooped to the twins' room and put them down for a nap. Dylan stopped in his office on the way down and when he finally reached the kitchen, April was explaining to Mrs. McWerren where they had been.

"It seems to be a well-constructed playground," she said.

"Oh my, yes," Mrs. McWerren said, "and pretty, too, all yellow and blue with that lovely merry-go-round thing. I always loved those when I was a girl, didn't you?"

Dylan was interested to see that April looked flustered. "Well, I—I don't actually know," she said. "My mother wasn't fond of playgrounds. She felt they were a waste of time."

"Oh, well, I suppose we all have our own feelings about what's fun and what isn't," Mrs. McWerren said, casting a questioning glance toward Dylan.

But he wasn't about to delve into April's past in front of another person. He knew what he was going to do, though.

"Come on," he said, reaching out for April's hand. "Mrs. McWerren, would you mind watching the boys while they sleep?"

"Not a bit."

"But where are we going?" April asked.

"To reinvent history," Dylan said with a sly whisper,

and he gave her hand a tug, trying not to notice how good her skin felt against his.

"This doesn't have anything to do with what I said about not visiting playgrounds, does it?" she asked, as he led her out across the grounds, through the gate and down the street in the same direction they'd walked just minutes ago.

He wasn't sure how to answer that just yet. She was beginning to tug at his hand with reluctance.

"There's nothing frightening about it, April."

"I'm not frightened. I'm just…you needn't feel sorry for me because I never rode on the merry-go-round."

"I don't," he lied. "But what if I told you that I don't have much experience of such things, either? My relatives were reluctant enough to take me in. They certainly didn't want to entertain me. None of them had any children my age."

April stopped moving. She looked up at Dylan, and he turned and began to walk backward slowly, taking both her hands in his, like a man skating on ice with his lady sliding after him. She took several reluctant steps with him.

"I don't think I'll be very good at this playing stuff."

"Never know until you try."

"You didn't hire me for this."

"It's important that you know how to have fun if you're going to take care of children."

"That's low," she said on a breath, "but probably true."

"I won't keep you long. Just long enough for both of us to get some experience. To raise a child, don't you think you should get into the mind of a child?"

"We're not raising children. We're just baby-sitting."

Everything she said was absolutely true, but Dylan

had some perverse and burning desire to rid himself of the picture of the little girl whose mother thought that she should not be allowed to visit playgrounds because it wasn't a serious enough pastime.

"Maybe we'll want to bring the boys to the playground again. We never got past the swings. Let's consider this research," he said, and he gave a gentle tug, bringing her closer to him. Close enough that he could have taken one step forward and taken her lips in a kiss.

If he were mad or wanted to go mad with desire.

Instead he turned and increased his pace. The playground was only a short distance away.

"I'll race you." Dylan let go of her hand and was off.

And just as he had hoped, April couldn't resist the challenge. Lightly she ran ahead straight through the gates and toward the merry-go-round. When she turned around, Dylan was right behind her, smiling.

"I suppose you think that you manipulated me into this?" she asked, raising her brows when they stopped.

"I would never dare to think I could manipulate a woman who has a double major in math and science. You're much too logical. I prefer to think that you finally saw the good sense in coming here."

"Good sense?"

"Of course. You represent a charity that helps children. Children like playgrounds, and sometimes playgrounds need to be upgraded. Every few years at least. You'll want Safe House to have the safest, most durable, most colorful and most fun equipment around, won't you?"

"Dylan, I have nothing to do with any of that."

"You could if you did your homework."

She crossed her arms indignantly, as she stepped up

onto the merry-go-round and Dylan began to gently and slowly push it. "I always do my homework," she said.

"I know. I've seen those journals. I've watched you research material for the boys. You could assist the Safe House Committee, but first you have to try out the latest equipment," and he gave the merry-go-round a big push as he stepped up behind April. She stumbled slightly, but he caught her around the waist and pulled her back against his chest. They leaned back against the center support and closed their eyes, letting the wind whip through their hair. Around and around the world flew by in a flash of vibrant green and energetic blue, but here on the merry-go-round April's body rested against his as he held her in his arms.

When the merry-go-round began to slow, Dylan let April go. He gazed down at her. She was looking half-dazed with wonder. "That was...exhilarating. I guess I never knew what I was missing. The merry-go-round, I mean," she said, and he knew that, like him, she was remembering that he had held her to keep her from falling.

"Let's do it again," he whispered, and this time she found a place to hold on to. He ran and ran and pushed the merry-go-round faster and faster before he jumped on and grabbed a handhold himself. This time the world was spinning so wildly that he didn't dare touch her.

Touching her had been a mistake. It had felt too good.

The minutes charged past with April's hair fluttering around her face, her eyes growing bright, her laughter joining with his.

"This is like flying on the ground. Maybe we should just be kids and let Mrs. McWerren take care of us," she said with a laugh.

"Well, at least we should do this again," Dylan admitted, with a laugh. "Who knew that baby-sitting would expose me to such new experiences?"

But he knew that as wonderful as this had been, there was a danger. He wanted to hear April's laughter again. He wanted to hold her against him while he lost his mind and the world turned into a blur of bright colors.

"Did you know that a baby's experiences can change the physiological development of his brain? It affects the electrical wiring between cells, and the better the wiring, the better the baby's life will be. So, singing to a child, sharing colors, textures and sounds with him helps form better connections that might not be made after age three. Wow, I didn't know that, did you?" April asked Dylan several days later. She was lying on her stomach on the floor of the sitting room, reading another book on baby care.

He looked up from his newspaper and smiled at her. "I sincerely hope that my brothers appreciate all the trouble you're going to for them."

She shook her head. "They're no trouble at all. They're just babies, and babies are a joy, they're a gift, they're so helpless. They need us to know these things, to be able to help them. And to protect them."

And suddenly the smile had disappeared from her voice, but when Dylan looked up she was hidden behind the pages of her book. Deliberately, he thought.

Slowly, he rose. He walked toward her and sat down on the floor beside her. He could see that she wasn't really looking at the book at all. It was time for some answers.

"April, did I do you a disservice when I hired you?" he wondered aloud.

She put the book down. "Disservice? You paid

twenty-five thousand dollars when I'd never even changed a diaper, Dylan.''

''That's not what I meant. You didn't really want this job. You wanted to tutor someone nearly full-grown or handle books for a business or work with computers. Babies weren't on your agenda, and I get the distinct impression that you have really good reasons for that.''

He held up his hand when she opened her mouth to speak. ''I'm not asking you to divulge your secrets,'' he said quietly. ''I'm just asking whether you regret being here.''

April stared up into Dylan's worried golden eyes. She did regret being here, all the time. Being with those adorable babies was both a joy and a knife slowly turning inside her. Being anywhere near Dylan was a most wonderful and awful temptation, a burning ache of forbidden desire. She didn't want to admit it, but she was practically trembling with the need for him to touch her again. She longed to have him place his lips against hers, to wrap his arms around her the way he had on the merry-go-round.

''I'm here,'' she said simply, ''and I'm staying until this job is done.''

Of course that wasn't what he'd asked.

''It hurts you sometimes to hold the boys. Jordie, especially. Maybe because he seems more sensitive?''

Okay, the man worked with complicated and technical security systems. He was a detail man. Of course he wouldn't miss much. And didn't she owe it to him to give him a bit of the truth? Maybe he wouldn't want her working with Jordie and Sam if he knew more about her.

She looked away. ''I hadn't been out of college long when I was swept off my feet by Nick Burnshaw. I thought I was in love. I thought *he* was in love, and then I found out I was pregnant and nobody was in love at all.''

"You have a child, then?" Dylan stared down at her flat abdomen. He reached out, nearly touching her there, before drawing his hand back. Of course a man with his reputed experience with women would know what a woman looked like after pregnancy. If he took her clothes off.

April swallowed hard and fought to get her thoughts on the right track. "No, I don't."

Dylan waited.

She struggled to find the right words. "Nick didn't want me. He thought that we were too different, and besides, he wasn't ready for fatherhood. I was upset. For three months I raged against my fate. I didn't want the baby, but I didn't want to get rid of it, either. And then slowly I accepted the fact that I was pregnant and that I would bear my child alone. Suddenly the baby was very important to me. Suddenly I wanted her more than anything else in the world.''

Something in her voice must have warned him what was to come. "You don't have to say any more, April," he said gently. "It's not my right to know."

"No, it's all right," she said. "Given the circumstances, you should know. Three weeks after I decided that I wanted my daughter, I miscarried. I lost her on a long, dark night I'll never forget.''

"And you think you were somehow to blame."

"I know enough biology to realize that miscarriage is quite common, but I also know something about psychology and the power of the mind over the body. I'm not sure if I didn't do things during that angry time that might have led to my miscarriage. I only know that it was terribly painful. She would have been three years old now.''

''The boys remind you of what you lost then?''

''Yes. And no. They're their own little selves. They're not Janie. And I don't begrudge them anything. How could I when they're so sweet and adorable and helpless? It's only that they make me think of what I threw away. But don't think I'm feeling sorry for myself. I made my choices in life, and some of them were bad. I know that there are a thousand reasons why Janie didn't survive, and most of them would have little to do with the mother's behavior or mental state.''

''But you still miss what you didn't get to have.''

She nodded slowly, and he tucked his hand gently beneath her chin.

''You'll have more babies someday,'' he said, ''with that man you're picking out for yourself. They won't be Janie, but they'll be yours.''

And his, he thought. Some man will make love with you, he'll plant his seed in you, he'll coach you through childbirth and he'll love you and your child.

''I'm not sure I want a child or that I can go through that again. I adore Sam and Jordie, I take joy in my students. I visit Safe House now and then to help out, and my heart breaks for every one of those kids, but to risk pregnancy and possible miscarriage again? I don't know if I want to try it.''

''But you definitely want a husband.''

She nodded. ''I want a companion. Someone just right for me. Someone matched perfectly to me.''

He knew that, but still her utter conviction hit him. Somewhere there was a man who fit her completely. It could never be him. Besides, when Valentine Enterprises went international, he would be away from Chicago for long periods of time. He'd be so busy that he might even forget how it had felt to stand on the merry-go-round with his arms around April's soft curves.

But for now he remembered that day and how much he'd wanted to ask her to come to his bed.

He still did.

Chapter Seven

"Do you think they'll have one?" April asked four days later as she and Dylan strolled into the new Tons of Toys store in the middle of town.

"If they don't, I pity the clerk who has to give you the bad news," Dylan said. "You've been almost more frantic than Sam since he lost his favorite rubber duck."

"But he liked it so much," April argued. "He took it into the bathtub. He slept with it. It made him feel safe and secure," she reminded Dylan, giving him a long, doleful look.

"Witch," he whispered with a smile. "You know that's my soft spot."

"Okay, I do. And you've been very good about this," she said soothingly. "Even though I know that you think it's silly to make such a big deal about one little rubber toy."

"I don't think it's silly. Not when I know it helps comfort him. I just don't want you and Sam to be disappointed if we can't find the very same one. We've already been to three toy stores. Do you think Sam will really know the difference if we get him something just a shade more yellow or one that isn't wearing a sailor hat?'' He smiled down at her.

"Actually, I'm worried that even if we find the same one he'll know it's not his. You know, the new toy smell and all.''

Dylan tucked a finger under her chin. "I tell you what. We'll just let Jordie mangle it a little and then it won't smell new anymore. Sam might even accept it.''

April considered that option. "You know, that might work. Jordie and Sam are very close. They cling to each other, little as they are.'' As he'd had no one to cling to when he was a child, she couldn't help think. He'd had nothing but his gadgets, which he loved.

She was glad that he hadn't guessed what she was really at here. Of course, she'd come for the rubber duck, but she was pretty sure Sam could be persuaded to transfer his affections. He was such an easygoing baby. What she really was looking for was some way to repay Dylan for what he was doing for the kids at Safe House and for the fact that he had taken her to the playground specifically to give her something that she had missed as a child.

She would have loved to return the favor by giving him what he'd missed as a child, too, but what he'd missed was what he didn't want. The closeness of another human being.

So, like Sam, she'd have to settle for second best. The perfect gadget. And since Dylan could easily afford any adult gadget available and probably had them all anyway, she was looking for something he might have missed as a child, because those people who should have cared about him hadn't.

It had to be something simple, not technological. He would know all those things. It should be old and yet new, something that would bring out the boy he'd once been. And there was a good chance she might find what she was looking for here, because this store had put out samples of most of the toys.

"Look at this," she said with a start as she picked up what looked to be six thin blocks of wood held together with ribbon. But when she grasped the bottom bit of wood, the whole row of blocks tumbled over each other in a quick and amazing waterfall of multi-colored ribbons and clacking wood. And when the tumbling was done, the row of blocks looked just the same as it had when it had started out.

"Intriguing," Dylan said. "It's called a Jacob's Ladder, according to the box. Let's see how it works." And he began to examine the bits of wood and ribbons.

"It's supposed to be fun," she said with a laugh.

"Could be. Probably is. It's rather ingenious," he agreed. "And this. Would you look at this. A tornado in a bottle," and he swirled the contents of the liquid-filled plastic tube around, creating what looked like a miniature tornado. "Think Sam would go for this?"

She crossed her arms.

He winked. "I know. A rubber duck. Like this one," and he plucked the very item from somewhere behind his back. He'd obviously picked it up several minutes ago.

April gave him the look she reserved for high school freshmen who thought they could outsmart her by forging their parents' names. "How long have you had that?"

He shrugged. "Not long. Come on, would you look at this?"

He dragged her over to a gigantic dollhouse. It was done up in lacy silver and pink with the most cunning miniature furniture April had ever seen. It was absolutely enchanting, and she would have loved to have taken the time to examine the details of each little room, but—

"This hardly seems like Sam's style," she said, giving him a long look. "Or Jordie's either, for that matter."

Dylan refused to look shamefaced, even though it was obvious that he had been edging her in that direction since they'd come into the store. "I'm sure that Viv would want her sons to grow up to be open-minded."

April couldn't help smiling. "You might be right, but maybe they'd like this better," and she knelt down on the alphabet-carpeted floor where a wonderfully intricate wooden train had been set up. Little wooden houses made of building blocks lined the tracks, and the train consisted of a multitude of red and blue and yellow cars. The track looped around the other toys, went over bridges, ran past crossings that could be manipulated by a touch of a button and past switching stations that could be hand-cranked. Little wooden people with smiles painted on their faces stood outside the houses and along the red-and-black train station.

"Wouldn't this make their eyes light up?" she asked, looking up at Dylan from beneath her lashes. She gave the train engine a push. It moved smoothly and easily around the track, stopping just short of where Dylan was standing. He dropped to one knee and gave the train a push himself.

He gave a low whistle. "This is…very nice. It's the kind of thing a kid could build on for years. I could see learning woodworking, so that you could add on buildings, maybe add trees. I could definitely see the boys owning one of these someday. What kid wouldn't fall in love? It's the kind of thing he could buy a piece at a time and save his money for.'' He brushed his fingertip over the curving lines of the bridge.

April held her breath, caught up in the clear amber of his eyes, the way his voice came soft and low, the way he looked thirteen rather than thirty all of a sudden. She was sure that he was imagining himself as a boy building on to this very train. And of course, it was much too expensive for her to afford, but maybe...a small plan began to form in her mind.

Dylan looked up. ''I do think that Sam would prefer the rubber duck for now, though. He's still a bit young for this.''

''You're probably right. We should just go with the duck.''

''He'll be beside himself with joy.''

She started to turn away toward the checkout counter, then realized that Dylan was holding more than just the rubber duck. Somewhere along the way he had also picked up a green frog which jumped and croaked when it was wound up. He had two clear balls that were filled with stars that glittered and turned when the ball was rolled. He had somehow managed to find two of the softest, most cuddly teddy bears that had ever been invented. A white one named Fuzz and a brown one named Binky.

April raised one brow. ''Been busy?''

''They're washable,'' he said, holding out the bears. ''I noticed that the boys tend to, um, christen most things with sticky hands.''

''And you noticed that they like soft, cuddly things, too, I'll bet,'' she said.

''Doesn't everyone?'' His eyes turned suddenly hot

and fierce. She was tempted to look down at her own thin body and point out that she wouldn't exactly be considered cuddly by most men, but somehow the thought of snuggling in tight against Dylan's body made her lose her voice.

And anyway, she must have just imagined that look in his eyes. He blinked and it was gone.

"We'd better get home," he said, and she realized that she was already responding to his house as if it were *her* home. That kind of thing had to stop.

"April?"

"Yes, we should go," she agreed.

When they moved up to the checkout stand, the cashier looked at their collection of toys and at the two of them. "You must be new parents," she said. "You seem so excited. That's always the way it is when it's your first. Is it?"

Dylan looked down into April's eyes. "Our first children?" He looked worried. No doubt he thought that the question might hurt her and bring back memories of the baby she'd never known. But she realized that just having confided in him the other night had made things easier. Besides, it was much too hard to explain their situation to strangers, as she'd said.

"Yes," she said softly as Dylan paid for their purchases. "Sam and Jordie are our first babies together."

It had been the right thing to say to the cashier. No more explanations were necessary, but her statement also implied, she realized, that she and Dylan might have more babies. They might find themselves together in a bed. Making love was a possibility.

April took a deep, shuddery breath. She cleared her throat. "That is, I mean—"

"Never mind, sweetheart," Dylan said, leaning close

like a lover or a mad-about-his-wife husband. "There are other customers waiting."

April looked over her shoulder and saw that there was, indeed, a line forming. She certainly didn't want to risk getting herself in any deeper under these circumstances.

"Let's go home now," she said quickly.

Too bad her voice had come out husky and that she had sounded like a woman eager to get her husband into a bed so that they could make more babies. The thought of being that intimate with Dylan made her blush and squirm. And worse.

"Best idea I've heard all day, love," Dylan said softly. He pulled her gently toward the door, and she dared a nervous glance up at him. His eyes looked a bit darker than normal, but other than that he looked calm. Not like he was dying to touch her.

For a second she felt disappointment. Then she gave herself a stern talking-to. Dylan was to be commended. Thank goodness at least one of them hadn't been thinking about beds.

But she wondered just what Dylan would do if he knew that she'd just envisioned herself naked in his arms.

His entire body was humming, Dylan thought as he walked down the street beside April on the way home. Or at least as close to her as he'd allow himself to get. After the conversation at the checkout counter, he didn't trust himself to get within touching distance. He didn't really even trust himself to look at her. He was that near the edge.

Still, as they passed the shops, he couldn't help sneaking a glance at her now and then—just to make sure that she was all right. And this time, when he turned, he saw that she wasn't. All right, that is.

Following her line of sight, he saw the children's clothing store coming up on the right. And there in the window was a little yellow dress with a white lacy bib. It was dainty, beautiful, just about the right size for a three-year-old girl.

When he turned back to April again, she was taking deep breaths, trying not to look at the dress.

"I'm fine," she said, her eyes sliding away from his. He could almost see the process, the way she was firming her chin, pulling her shoulders back, adding a little more steel to her backbone. No doubt she didn't want him to see her upset.

No doubt he didn't give a damn. If she needed comfort, he was darn well going to provide it.

"You don't have to be fine," he said gently.

Carefully he stepped between her and the window. He let the package he was carrying slide to the ground. He reached out and took her in his arms, he slid his hand up beneath her hair, he pulled her into his body and rocked her.

She came to him easily. She nestled in his arms, ducking her head and nuzzling deeper into his body. He kissed the top of her honeysuckle-scented hair.

A long shudder ripped through her.

He folded her closer still.

They stood there for long minutes until he felt her heartbeat slowing, her trembling lessen.

Finally she pulled away, untucked her head and looked up at him. "Thank you," she said, her voice a trembly whisper. "This isn't the first time this has happened, of course, but it—it's getting easier. You've helped make it easier. Thank you."

Dylan was shaking his head. "Don't thank me, and don't be ashamed for wanting to know what she would have been like. Things catch us by surprise sometimes. Right when we think we have everything sorted out. That's natural."

She nodded slightly and smiled up at him. "I think you're right. Still, I *will* thank you for being here for me. You're a good man, Dylan."

He smiled at her and wanted nothing more than to bring back her light. "Tell Mrs. McWerren I'm a good man, will you? She thinks I'm wicked."

April's smile grew. "She thinks you're devilish and a flirt, but you're still a good man, and I'm sure she would agree."

He grinned. "Trying to spare my feelings? I guess that makes you a good woman, April."

"Well, aren't we lucky, then?" she teased, and he knew then that he had her back. A passerby jostled him and he caught her close to keep her from falling.

She clutched at his arms, her softness striking him, and when she looked up there was an awareness of him in her eyes. He was no longer her comforter, but a man once again. She cleared her throat. "I suppose we should stop blocking the sidewalk and go home now," she said, peering around him.

"We'll take it slow." He retrieved his package, and they began to walk.

But this time it was different. For him, anyway. They were touching now. And only a moment ago, she had been pressed against him, her body warm and soft and pliant.

He glanced at her briefly and saw that there was soft color in her cheeks. She looked away quickly, and he realized that she probably had been thinking the same thing, too.

Not good.

"What do you think of that?" he asked suddenly, pointing out an ornate cuckoo clock in a shop they were passing.

She smiled in relief. "I think I'm not the cuckoo clock type. I have enough trouble dealing with my own personal doubts without having a bird telling me that I'm nuts every hour."

He grinned at her teasing tone, but she was already getting into the game.

"How about that?" she asked, motioning to a fountain, a woman pouring water from a jar.

Dylan grimaced. "Seen it too many times. Now maybe if the strap of her dress were drooping a bit more..."

April chuckled and hit him. "You're not taking the game seriously."

"All right then, how about that?" A perfectly matched set of amethysts gleamed in a jeweler's window.

She gave him an "are you kidding" look. "Do I look like a complete fool?" she asked.

He grinned. "I have it on good authority that you are highly intelligent."

"Then why bother even asking what I think? Any sane woman loves amethysts."

He studied the jewels carefully, an idea forming in his mind.

She tugged on his sleeve and pulled his face close. "And don't even think what you're thinking. Just because I fell apart back there, I do not need jewels to

cheer me up. I don't care if you're richer than Bill
Gates.''

Damn. Caught.

With a last look of regret, Dylan walked on with her.
She pointed out a sculpture that looked like a man with
a pineapple on his head. He showed her a hat covered
in artificial birds.

''Very Carmen Miranda in an aviary sort of way,''
she agreed.

Their gazes zipped back and forth from store to store.
They were almost at the end of the shopping area and
only a short few blocks from Dylan's home when Dylan
turned to the next store window. ''What do you
think—'' he began to say automatically, still in midturn.

He felt April stiffen beside him. She stopped. So did
he.

The shop sold lingerie. The outfit suspended from a
tiny velvet hanger was black lace and air, dipping low
in the front and high at the thighs. The straps were made
to slide off the shoulders easily. There was no back to
speak of.

And there was no need to ask what anyone thought,
because all Dylan could think of was April's body dis-
played in a small scrap of black lace and air, and himself
sliding the straps down her shoulders as he dipped his
head to nuzzle the tops of her breasts. He could almost
imagine sliding his hands up her long naked thighs to
settle at the place where lace met bare skin.

And he knew that April was aware of his thoughts.

He was also aware that in his present aroused state he
had no business being with her or even being in public.

She didn't object when he tugged on her hand and
started down the sidewalk at a quick clip. Her curls

bounced as she quickened her steps, and he thought of blond curls spilling over his chest.

He lengthened his stride and all he could think of was the length of her legs beneath her rose-red dress.

She rushed forward to match his pace and he could only think of matching his rhythm to hers as he moved inside her.

He couldn't reach the house quickly enough, and April seemed to feel the same.

Opening the door, he stepped aside to let her inside.

He fully intended to make a quick excuse and retreat to the solitude of his office or a cold shower.

But as she moved past him, he caught her scent, and his will snapped.

"April," he said, his voice too deep and thick.

She turned, she looked at him, and then he stepped close. He leaned over and claimed her lips.

She was warm and sweet and wild in his arms. Her slender arms snaked around him, her mouth moved beneath his own, parting for him as he nudged her to open.

His hands were in her hair, sliding down, fitting her to him. He was so hard, so damn in need of her, more urgent than he could remember ever being.

"Come closer," he urged and he reeled her in. Her breasts brushed against him, driving him mad. Her hips fit against his.

Somewhere he heard a door creaking, a child murmuring.

And he realized that he was practically dragging April to the floor.

"Hell," he said, forcing himself to pull back slightly even as the ache in his body intensified.

He looked down into her dazed violet eyes, saw the evidence of his kisses on her swollen lips, a slight redness on her cheek where his five o'clock shadow had scraped her.

"I should say I'm sorry," he began, barely able to speak, still not in control of his body.

She took a breath to speak, and he touched his fingertips to her red lips. "I wanted you very badly, and as I said, I'm sure that I should say I'm sorry, but I'm not sure that I wouldn't have lost complete control if I hadn't at least tasted you. We're probably all right now. I'm... I can step away."

And he did. She still hadn't spoken.

"Maybe the next time you go into your perfect mate program you should make a note that your perfect man would be someone who doesn't maul you," he said solemnly.

For long seconds they just looked at each other. "It didn't feel like mauling," she finally said on a whisper.

He frowned, prepared to point out the bare facts to her. "Perhaps you weren't paying attention."

"You had my complete attention. It *didn't* feel like mauling," she insisted. "It felt indescribably wonderful."

He wanted to beat his head on a wall or roar with frustration.

"But still, Dylan," she said, shaking her head. "You're right that we can't do this and that I should think about the future. I think I'm going to go do just that. As soon as I check on the boys."

And she slipped away from him. To go back to her job with Sam and Jordie. And to contact the other men in her life, he supposed.

The perfect men.

In a few seconds all that remained was the womanly scent of her. He breathed it in and resolved to start behaving more like an employer and less like a lover. Especially since there was no future in being April's lover.

And since he didn't want a future with a woman at all.

But fifteen minutes later, after he had dismissed Mrs. McWerren and stopped in to see the boys, only to discover that they were napping peacefully, he found himself headed toward the study where April was searching for her perfect man.

Chapter Eight

It had been all she could do to check on Sam and Jordie, to pretend everything was fine when she spoke to Mrs. McWerren. Of course, things were not fine, and she didn't need the speculative look the woman gave her to know that.

Her heart was still pounding, her body was throbbing, no doubt her hair was a mess. Her lips were sensitive and there was no telling what they looked like. In fact, April thought, her entire body was probably a dead give-away as to what she and Dylan had been doing. Or about to do.

It had been overwhelming, mad, glorious to feel his lips moving over hers, his fingertips working magic on her skin.

It had possibly been the most foolhardy thing she had ever done in her life. So it was with the greatest of haste that April made her way to her laptop.

"Way past time to get on with my life." She called up a file with notes on all the things she felt she could bring to a relationship. Everything seemed to be in order there.

She clicked on another file that showed what she was looking for in a relationship. Everything still fit as far as she could tell. Of course she wanted a man of science or numbers. And naturally, she would like a man who understood the importance of building a relationship on mutual interests. A simple man physically, not too tall. Definitely below six feet, she thought with a frown. A man who wouldn't overwhelm her senses. Only average in looks. A man who wanted a quiet, settled life with no surprises, and who was willing to wait to decide if he ever wanted children. A man who would like a friend and not expect too much in the way of passion or romance.

It all read correctly. Just as it had yesterday.

But today her lips ached, and a man had come along and made her want to do things she'd only read about in books.

And that was just the kind of thinking she couldn't afford to indulge in. It meant that she was acting like her grandmother all over again.

"It's not going to happen," she told herself fiercely. "What isn't?"

She turned to see Dylan in the doorway, his arms crossed as he leaned casually against the doorframe.

No question, she was blushing. "I was just thinking out loud. Can I help you?"

He tilted his head. "Maybe. You know my natural curiosity about technological issues. I'm interested in this program you've created. Care to show me how it works?"

For an instant she was embarrassed. This would be, after all, her personal life laid bare for Dylan to see.

But then she brushed that thought aside. Those kinds of thoughts were the very things that had been causing her problems lately. She was a woman of math and science and she had used her skills to create this program. It was a nifty bit of programming, too, nothing to be ashamed of. Besides, she and Dylan might have shared a brief and ill-advised moment of passion, but she had herself under control now.

And if she wanted to put the incident behind her, she had to act as if nothing had happened. Maybe nothing had. The kiss had probably been routine to Dylan.

"Of course, you may look at my matchmaking program. It's fairly simplistic in terms of data entry. I take certain traits and translate them into alpha and numeric equivalents. Other people do the same, and the program looks for patterns. Of course, it takes a human element to sort things out and choose which candidates of the ones presented are actually best suited to their tastes, but I haven't experienced too many glitches."

She was certainly experiencing an awareness of Dylan as he moved to stand beside her, though. April frowned at the way her breath seemed to be fighting her control.

"Show me," he said, leaning nearer. His breath whispered gently past her ear.

"Here." Her voice broke slightly and she cleared her throat. She flexed her fingers to keep them from trembling before she placed them on the keyboard. "Here are the things I can bring to a relationship." She fought self-consciousness as she showed him what she had entered into the computer.

Dylan tried to keep his eyes and his attention on the screen, not the woman. He really was interested in what she had come up with, although he wasn't sure if his reasons for being interested were as simple as he wished.

He *was* sure about one thing. Having his lips this close to her pale, graceful neck made him want to spin her chair around, to kneel before her, lean in close and touch his lips to the fragile flesh of her throat.

He swallowed hard and blinked as a list of the things April felt she could bring to a relationship spilled onto the screen.

"Degrees in math and science," he read. "Graduated magna cum laude. Three years of teaching at the high school level. Member of the International Association of Science Teachers, President of the Chicago branch of Amateur Mathematicians. Ability to prepare gourmet dinners, sew if necessary and run a household. In excellent health."

"There, that's me," April said, reaching for the keyboard. "Now I'll show you what I'm looking for."

But Dylan reached out and gently closed his fingers around hers, stopping her.

"That's not you," he said.

She looked up indignantly. "Of course it is. All of those things are true."

"I know."

She shook her head, clearly confused.

"What about the fact that you care about lost boys, those at Safe House? How about your ability to soothe the tears of brokenhearted babies? The fact that you're patient, so patient that when Jordie slopped pureed pears over you three times this week, you didn't yell. And how about the fact that you love amethysts and lacy dollhouses?"

"I hardly think the fact that I like amethysts and dollhouses is relevant to a relationship."

He crossed his arms. "It could be. A husband should

give his wife gifts now and then. And I don't mean things that are floating in formaldehyde, either.''

She smiled at that. ''Have you been reading my journal?''

He smiled, too. ''No, you might have mentioned it to the boys one day when Sam was studying bugs in the garden. I seem to recall that a little boy in third grade gave you a very dead but well-preserved grasshopper.''

''Sweet of him,'' she admitted. ''For a third grader, anyway.''

''Do you still have it?'' he asked, raising a brow, wondering why he should feel even the slightest bit of interest in whether she had kept something given to her by a boy in third grade.

April smiled. ''No. I wasn't that interested in science during those years, and besides, he moved on to another girl the next week. I think he gave her a dead mouse. Lucky me.''

''Perhaps you should specify that you don't want any men who hand out biological matter as gifts.''

''Good idea,'' she said with a chuckle.

''When *did* you get into the science thing?'' he asked, pulling a chair up and sitting beside her.

It was a logical question, but April seemed to move behind a mask at his words. Finally, she shrugged. ''My grandmother was alive then. She was…well, I guess you could say that she was a woman who was ruled by her emotions. She was a romantic, and after my grandfather died just after I was born, she was always either falling madly in love and soaring to the stars, falling out of love, or being dropped by someone who no longer loved her, a fact which sent her whole world plummeting. She was that way until the day she died. It upset and angered my mother, who told me there was a better way to live. It was true, too, because she and my father had a marriage based simply on mutual interests, and they had a very nice relationship.

"While my father was alive, my mother's life was a steady hum of contentment, not a rocket to the moon followed by a meteor plummeting to the ground every other week. Her marriage wasn't all highs and lows the way my grandmother's apparently had been. Anyway, after a particularly bad summer with my grandmother when I was twelve, my mother started enrolling me in summer science and math classes. I was good at it and I liked the sense of order in my life. My mother was right. There is a better way. Building a relationship based on logic makes more sense than following the unreliable dictates of one's emotions."

Dylan's mind was aflame. He wanted to take April into his arms and tell her that she shouldn't feel guilty for having loved and lost even though he suspected her mother had told her something different. He wanted to hold her and show her that her grandmother had been right. Passion wasn't something to discard so easily. But that would be unforgivable, wouldn't it? He could only offer her moments. In just a few weeks, their paths would part. Throwing passion that couldn't last into the mix would be the greatest of mistakes. It would hurt her more than she'd already been hurt.

"That's quite a program," he said quietly, searching for some way to change the subject and calm his own passions.

She smiled slightly. "I like it. It does what I want it to do."

"Unlike people," he suggested.

April lifted a delicate shoulder. "I suppose that could be true. I just like the simplicity and logic of it."

"And has it produced any results?"

A pale pink blush climbed up her throat. "I'm not sure. It's produced candidates. I only responded to one of them, but I haven't had an answer yet."

She took a visible breath. Her color deepened as she pulled her shoulders back in a determined line. "Perhaps we should see," she said.

He wasn't sure he liked that. If she received an answer to her queries, it would be personal, private, a message from a man who was interested in pursuing a relationship with her. But it was so obvious that she was trying to show that this process was pure logic, no passion, that any response other than a positive one would be calling the lady a liar.

"Let's see what you have," he said, his voice low.

She clicked on a few keys, called up her e-mail. Several messages came in.

"These two are business. School stuff," she said, scrolling past them. "This one, though…" Her fingers froze on the mouse.

Dylan wanted to look away. Obviously he ought to pretend he hadn't seen anything, but when she'd clicked on the message, the preview box had come up and the first words on the page had practically leapt out.

I've been watching you, April.
It appears you're enjoying your stay with your billionaire, but be careful. He might not be as patient as I was about claiming you for a prize. Not all men know how to wait for the mouse to come to them.

Dylan grasped the back of her chair. His fingers dug into the soft padding. He could feel her body, tense and stiff, as she sat there, her fingers still clenched around the mouse.

"It appears your other bidder is still upset," Dylan said tightly, scanning down to the bottom of the message.

"It must have been him," April said. "I thought I felt someone watching me when I was out with the boys the other day."

Dylan slowly spun the chair around. He dropped to his knees and took April's cold hands in his own.

"You didn't tell me?" he asked softly.

She shook her head. "I convinced myself that I was imagining things. I guess I was wrong. I should... I should—"

"No, you shouldn't. I'll take care of this."

"What will you do?"

"Don't worry about it."

She placed a gentle hand on his arm. "It's my problem. I'll worry if you get involved."

"I'm not going to threaten the man with a weapon, April, but I'll get results. I've learned how to deal with bullies over the years."

She raised one brow at that.

He shrugged. "There were times when I was staying with my relatives that I was clearly the outsider. It made me a target. Once I even had an uncle who decided that I'd make a good punching bag."

"What happened?"

"I enlisted the aid of a kid several years my senior who had taken martial arts lessons. He taught me enough to ensure that no one would be able to mess with me again."

"And he agreed to do this because..."

Dylan grinned. ''There are advantages to being wealthy with a genetic predisposition to knowing how to make a deal. We came to terms.''

She opened her mouth. To ask more, no doubt, but he didn't want to tell her more. She was too soft and sweet to be comfortable with what the struggle for survival had led him to do at times in his younger days.

''I'll take care of it, April. I promise you that. You're doing me a great favor here with the boys. I owe you.''

She started to object. He stared her directly in the eyes.

''You *are* helping me. I'll see to Jason.''

Finally she nodded, though he thought her capitulation was somewhat reluctant. ''You'll need his e-mail address,'' she said, and she printed it out.

He took it. There was no point in telling her that he didn't intend to send Jason Olney an e-mail. Nothing but face-to-face contact would do in this case.

April was getting ready for bed a few hours later when her computer told her that she had more mail. Her heart started to pound. Obviously Dylan hadn't had time to contact Jason yet.

The fact that he was going to contact him at all didn't feel right. Dylan hadn't really wanted to hire her. She had been thrust into his life because of Jason in the first place.

''*And* because Dylan is a good man,'' she whispered to herself. Most people wouldn't have gotten involved. Now she was involving him still more, entangling him in her life.

She didn't want that. Not for him. He had his own life to live, his own priorities, and he'd made it clear that while he desired her, he wasn't looking for anything more.

That should have served as a warning that sent all desire for him fleeing. It should have called up all the times her mother told her, "Don't fall in love. Only idiots choose love over common sense. Love breeds discontent." And she had remembered all her mother's good advice, but somehow whenever she was near Dylan, her mind seemed to turn to porridge.

Still, she knew that dragging Dylan deeper into her problems wouldn't be wise. What if Jason tried to hurt Dylan? She couldn't let that happen.

"So open your mail, coward," she whispered. "Deal with this situation yourself. You can tell Dylan that everything is taken care of."

She jerked her head in response, clicked on the mouse and went into her in-box. There was only one message.

It wasn't from Jason.

She read the text.

Dear April,
Sorry to take so long getting back to you. I was out of town for a few days. Will be in Chicago in two days. You sound like an interesting woman who meets all of my requirements for a mate.
Would like to meet you and have lunch or something.
Let me know.

Greg Larraby

April blinked at the wording. That she met all of his requirements for a mate sounded so nakedly blunt and cold. But wasn't that what she wanted?

"Exactly," she muttered. "Of course it is. I guess I should go see if Dylan can spare me for a few hours."

Throwing on a long white robe over her floor-length white eyelet nightgown, she crept out into the hallway. She had passed Dylan's room many times. She had never gone near it. For half a second, she hoped that he was already asleep, but the light beneath the door said otherwise. Tentatively she raised her fist and rapped lightly on the door.

A mouse could do better, she chided herself and hit the door harder.

Just then the door slid open and there she stood, arm raised to Dylan as though she intended to beat on his chest.

She willed herself to look away from his chest, but when she tried, her gaze couldn't find a decent resting place. His amber eyes made her breath catch, his jaw was shadowed and made for touching, his lips lifted in a sexy smile.

The eyes would have to do, even though they tended to set something to smoldering inside her every time she looked directly at him.

Dylan's smile faded slightly. "You look distressed, April," he said, drawing her inside. "Is there a problem with the boys?"

"No, not the boys. Me. That is, I just wanted to let you know that I received a message from my first candidate. He says he'd like to get together with me the day after tomorrow for lunch or something. Could I... Would you mind if I take a few hours off?"

Dylan stared down at her, a frown on his lips.

"I'm sorry. I probably shouldn't have asked," she began, "but I thought that perhaps Mrs. McWerren would be available."

"Lunch or *something?*" Dylan asked. "What's 'or something'?"

Oh, was that all? He thought Greg might be implying something illicit?

"I'm sure he simply meant that I might have something else I'd rather do," she said. "Like take in a museum or a trip to the library."

"You're kidding. You really believe that?"

She smiled, relief gushing through her. "Of course that's all it is."

His brows drew together in a scowl. He muttered something about "innocence" and "men."

April placed a hand on his arm, and his bare flesh heated beneath her fingertips. She fought the urge to slide her hand farther up, to touch his chest.

"I'll be fine," she whispered, and she wasn't sure if she was talking about her lunch date with Greg or this moment.

Dylan blew out a breath. "I don't have any right to stop you, but I think you're making a mistake being so trusting. Have him come here. I'd like to meet him."

She opened her mouth to object. It was clear that Dylan wanted to protect her, and she didn't need protecting. Certainly not from someone like Greg. She had all his references, she'd done her homework, but maybe this was the smartest thing to do. Dylan dealt with men all the time, he knew them. And when Greg showed up, Dylan would see that everything was fine. It would reassure him that she was safe.

She wanted to do something nice for him.

"We'll meet here," she agreed.

A short time later, she lay in bed trying to make plans for what she and Greg would do after their lunch together. And then she realized that she was cradling her hand to her heart. The hand that she had touched Dylan with only moments before.

Thank goodness Greg was coming. There was nothing like the prospect of the perfect man to help her forget that her lips still ached for Dylan to kiss her again.

Chapter Nine

"Hell and damnation!" Dylan slammed the receiver back onto the telephone and stared at it as if it were his worst enemy. Well, close enough. He'd been on the trail of Jason Olney and he'd discovered some things which might prove useful, but the man had slipped away just as he was closing in. That couldn't be allowed to happen. The viper had been following April.

"Leave her alone and I might leave you alone, Olney," Dylan whispered, swiping his hand over his eyes.

He took a few deep breaths, pushing himself back from his desk. The mere fact that he had taken to talking to himself and slamming telephones around was proof enough that he was getting in too deep with April. Normally, he could be a ruthless businessman, but he was never impatient. Now he could barely wait to mix it up with Jason Olney.

April was definitely having a strange effect on him. Getting him to sing to the boys at night. Making him feel as if he wanted to protect her.

Thank goodness the days were slipping away. Soon April would be gone. Probably off to marry this Greg guy who was due to show up today.

The man had better be a perfect gentleman. One word that implied that he intended anything other than lunch, like…

Like kissing her the way *he* had just the other day? Like dreaming of her naked in his arms the way Dylan had been doing ever since she got here?

A low growl rumbled from Dylan's throat and he reached for the telephone, determined to beat on something. Might as well find Olney and take out some of his frustrations.

"Dylan?"

April's voice sounded softly, and then she was standing in the doorway of his office, her blond curls framing her face like a halo, an angel-eyed cherub tottering on either side of her.

"I just wanted you to know that I was going to take the boys outside to play. They were cooped up yesterday because of the rain, and Mrs. McWerren won't be by until much later. You asked me to let you know if we left the house, so I'm," she smiled, "letting you know."

Automatically he rose. "I'll come with you."

"Oh Dylan, no, you have work. I didn't mean to disturb you. I just…"

It didn't matter if she'd meant to disturb him or not. She *did* disturb him, every second of every day. Which was just plain wrong. Soon, he'd be far away from her, traveling the world, on his own again. The way he liked it.

But for now, she had a jerk spying on her, so the fact that spending hours just out of kissing reach of April would be exquisite torture was irrelevant.

"No problem," he said as smoothly as he could manage. "I could use some fresh air myself."

And if Olney was in the vicinity trying to get near her, heaven help the man.

April was looking at him with raised brows. She glanced at the pile of papers on his desk.

He hazarded a smile. "It's just paper, April. It'll keep." And he left all of it behind, leading her and the boys out into the sunshine.

"Come on, guys," April said to Sam and Jordie. "Let's see if there's anything new in the garden. Well, look at this," and she plopped down onto the ground, her pale yellow skirts billowing around her. Jordie and Sam crowded in close, their little eyes round with wonder at what April was showing them.

"Raspberries," she said, setting her cute little glasses on her nose and pointing to the delicate fruit. "Did you know that there are over two hundred different species of raspberries, but only two are grown on any large scale? The plant used to be used for medicine—you, know, like in raspberry leaf tea—long before the fruit became popular. Isn't that interesting?"

Jordie and Sam stared at her blankly, clearly entranced but clueless.

And then she grinned and hugged them close. "And you know what else is cool about raspberries? They're sweet, just like you two." And she popped a berry in her mouth to demonstrate, then broke one in two and slipped a small piece in each of the boys' mouths.

Sam's eyes lit up like twinkling festival lights. "Eat," he said.

"Guh," said Jordie and he opened his mouth like a baby bird begging for more.

"Yes, they *are* very good, aren't they? Okay, one

more," April agreed, giving them another taste. "But we can't have more than that. I'm not sure if raspberries are good for babies with all those little seeds. Besides, the gardener might have our heads if we ate all of his fruit. Right?"

The boys were too busy feeling the ripe berries on their tongues to answer, but they looked as if they agreed, Dylan decided. Moreover, they looked happy, and so did April. He was suddenly amazed at how much he had lucked out when he'd bid on her at the auction. He might have ended up with Agnes somebody, and she would no doubt have been helpful, but would she have even considered talking to the boys about topics that were well over their heads as if they understood? Would she be brushing her lips against their foreheads or swinging them around one at a time in big, dipping circles that made Sam laugh outright and even made Jordie chuckle until all of them were lying on their stomachs on the bare ground, dizzy and resting?

"Of course not," he whispered, as he watched from several feet away, content to maintain his post as watchdog. At least he didn't think so. The bare ground part would most likely have stopped Agnes. And she probably wouldn't have approved of, or even thought of the sneaking-raspberries-out-of-the-garden part. And maybe she wouldn't have looked at the boys as if they were the most beautiful things she'd ever seen—the way April was looking at them now.

"You guys are the best. Did you know that?" April asked, hugging each of them close. "Not even one drop of juice on your clothes today. Not that I would have minded if you'd done that, you know. Messes just happen when you're eighteen months old. I realize that. But you're so good, you're so sweet."

"Sweet," Sam said, pointing to the raspberries.

"Yes, hon, just like that," April said. "Now. Who's up for a good Frisbee toss?"

Jordie whooped and held up his arms overhead. "Frizz," he proclaimed as April pulled a round orange disc out of the bag she'd been carrying.

"How about we get Dylan to play, too," she suggested, and both boys looked toward him.

Automatically Dylan felt his chest constrict. Watching the three of them was one thing. Easy. Enjoyable, like a good movie, but more and more lately he was finding it hard to come into the inner circle. This was almost over. Getting too involved wouldn't be wise.

Besides, if he was playing with the three of them, he might not notice if Jason should show up.

"I don't think that's a good idea today," he said, crossing his arms. "I'm enjoying the show."

April raised one brow. "I know what you're doing, you know, and you don't have to. Jason is a jerk," she said, getting right to the point, "but I'm not afraid to talk about him, so there's no point in trying to protect me from the obvious. I know you just came out with us to make sure he didn't come around, but the man is hardly likely to do anything on Valentine property. Come on, Dylan, the boys want you here. I want you here."

Her voice was a low invitation. Under other circumstances, he would have taken it as a sensual invitation to come to her bed, but he knew that while there was undoubtedly something wild and untamed that passed between the two of them, what she meant was something else. She had been bothered by his admissions about being unwanted and punished by his relatives as a child. It had been obvious, just as it was now obvious that she was trying to take care of him as well as the boys. She didn't want him to be an outsider. How could he tell her that being an outsider was what had saved his sanity all those years ago? And holding on to that outsider status, nurturing it, was what kept him whole today?

He couldn't tell her. "All right, count me in. But just for today," he said.

Surely he could handle this without breathing in the baby scent of his brothers too much or getting in so deep that he would remember those innocent wide eyes and miss them when they were gone. And maybe if he was careful, he could keep his hands from itching to catch April close for a slow, hot kiss.

And maybe I'm going nuts, he thought. But he still joined the game.

"Rolling it would probably work better at this stage. I don't think they can catch yet," April suggested, so the boys toddled around, throwing themselves on the rolling disk and laughing when they managed to trap it. Dylan tried a gentle toss to April. She crossed her eyes and wrinkled her nose at him.

"For all intents and purposes, I have the athletic abilities of an eighteen-month-old, I'll have you know," she told him, but she reached out and made a try for it, missing by a mile and ending up on the ground in a tangle of frothy skirts and long, exposed legs.

"Very nice," he said, gazing at her legs.

"But I missed it." She climbed to her knees and shoved her mass of curls out of her eyes.

"So you did." He smiled, and she blushed a pretty pink. In the next second, she had sailed the Frisbee directly at him, low. Caught unaware, Dylan still managed to drop to one knee and snag it. He held it up triumphantly as April applauded and Sam toddled over, his rosebud lips raised for a kiss.

For several seconds, Dylan merely stared at the little boy, aghast.

"Sam," April said, moving forward. No doubt to salvage the little boy's feelings, Dylan thought with a savage twist of his gut. What kind of man would turn away from a sweet child looking for affection, he wondered, seeing the confused look that began to dawn in Sam's blue eyes.

"I'll take him," April said gently, standing at Dylan's side now, but he held out one hand to stop her. Awkwardly, he lifted Sam and kissed his baby brother. Immediately Sam smiled.

Dylan realized that Jordie, as always, was waiting quietly, patiently on the sidelines, so he turned and held his arms out to the child. With a shy smile, Jordie tumbled forward, nearly falling into Dylan's arms as he was caught and pulled close. Dylan kissed Jordie as well, then put the little boy back in his place on the grass.

April's eyes were misty. "That was very well done."

"It doesn't come naturally to me, and probably never will. I don't invite closeness."

She nodded. "I know. It's okay."

But it wasn't, because he desperately wanted to know what it would be like to let her in for just a second or two. But not like Sam or Jordie. No kisses, because touching April was complicated, maddening, it was a burning deep within him, and that meant he couldn't give in to it.

"One more game?" he asked as casually as he could, holding out the Frisbee with a smile.

She smiled back and held out her hand, but at that

moment a car rounded the bend and pulled into the long drive. An unfamiliar car.

"That must be Greg," she said, and he could hear the tension in her voice.

"No," he wanted to say, but this was what she wanted. He had to want it for her as well.

"I'll take the boys in so that you can go meet him," he suggested.

For half a second, he thought he saw panic in her eyes, but then she nodded and raised her chin. "Yes. Thank you." Her voice was faint but her eyes were determined. Well, he supposed she deserved to be a bit nervous. She would find out now if her program had worked its magic.

And he would find out what kind of a man she really wanted.

Not a good way to think. "Come on, guys." He lifted Sam and Jordie into his arms.

Inside the house, the phone was ringing. Quickly he placed the boys inside their protected play area, then picked it up.

For several seconds, he heard nothing but breathing. Then the phone went dead in his hand.

Dylan stared at it. Could have been a wrong number. Or it could have been Olney. He didn't know, but he resolved to find out. Later. Just as soon as he knew that April was safely back from her date.

He wondered if Greg Larraby was going to kiss her and if *he* was going to be able to refrain from hitting the man.

Of course, he was. April wanted the guy.

But her perfect man had better give her perfect treatment.

* * *

Well, here she was. Dylan had gone inside and it had been all April could do to keep from chasing after him.

"Silly, this is what you wanted," she told herself. And it was. When Greg stepped from his car, he looked exactly like his picture. Sandy brown hair, nondescript brown eyes, average height. Nice, but not too nice.

She forced a smile and stepped forward. "Hi, I'm April."

"Greg," he said. "Are you ready to go?"

No. Panic set in. Probably because he was a total stranger, she told herself even though she knew it was more.

"Why don't you come inside for a while?"

He looked at her strangely, and she had an awful feeling. He thought she was inviting him to do something she had no intention of doing.

"I'd like you to meet my friends," she clarified, "and I can't just leave without telling my boss I'm going."

A sense of relief slipped through her when he agreed and turned to follow her.

"Dylan?" she called as they went inside.

She peered off in the direction of the parlor where the boys would most likely be playing, but as she leaned in that direction, Dylan came around the corner, a baby in each arm. He looked so tall and handsome, his dark hair mussed where Sam and Jordie had tangled their fingers in it.

He looked like a father, like a husband, like a man a woman would wait all day to make love with once the children were in bed.

That would never be. And she was supposed to be getting to know her perfect man. Greg was supposed to be getting to know her. That would happen, just as soon as she felt comfortable and safe.

April stretched her arms out toward Dylan. "Here, let me help."

He raised one brow. "I thought you were going."

"In a minute or two," she agreed. "Dylan, I'd like you to meet Greg Larraby. Greg, this is Mr. Valentine. I thought we might all sit and talk for a while until the boys are settled down. You've never stayed alone with them, you know," she told Dylan.

"That's true. Could be a heck of a disaster," he said, a wicked gleam in his eyes. "Nice to meet you, Larraby. I hear you're…"

April held her breath, sure that Dylan was going to say "the perfect mate."

"I hear you're interested in science and math."

Greg seemed to relax. He meekly followed April and Dylan into the blue parlor where the two of them sat down on the sofa, each with a baby on their lap. April motioned Greg to a high-backed chair. He eyed Dylan with interest.

"Actually, I'm a physics professor. What about yourself?"

"I own a company that installs high-tech security systems."

"Useful."

"Most people think so."

April watched the two men eyeing each other. She winked at Sam, who chortled and hugged her. Jordie, uncharacteristically, edged in to demand a hug for himself.

And then they went back to Dylan, asking him for a hug.

And back to April.

In the meantime, Greg was leaning back and forth, trying to get a good view of Dylan. When Dylan winked at Sam and blew a raspberry on his tummy, making him squeal, Greg apparently decided the man couldn't be all that high-powered or interesting. He turned to April.

"Did you read that article in *Sci-View* the other day about loop quantum gravity?"

Ordinarily she would have, but she'd been so busy with the boys—all three of them—that she hadn't gotten around to reading much at all.

She shook her head.

Greg looked slightly miffed. Then he glanced at Dylan as if he might have read the article.

"Sorry, my head was in the *Journal* and the latest baby manual last week."

Greg's brows drew together, but he nodded. "How about the one in *Math-netics Gazette* on Zeno's Paradoxes?"

"No," April said sadly. She'd brought him all this way. It seemed impolite to have failed to do her homework.

Dylan shook his head as well.

Sam laughed and moved over to Greg, clearly expecting to be picked up and hugged. Greg leaned so that he could see April.

"How about the 'Nanophysics Update' in *The Monthly Science Review?*"

A deep sigh of frustration escaped April. Was Dylan actually stifling a laugh? She gave him "the look," but he only smiled innocently, sexily at her.

She quickly looked away and gave Greg a friendly smile. Sam returned to her and she cuddled him close, wrapping her arms around him.

"No?" Greg asked, sounding slightly depressed. "You didn't read that one, either?"

"No," she confessed, "but—" But what? "But I read

the one in *Research Quest* last month on the latest news in machine self-replication.''

''Yeah?''

Guilt attacked her. Greg looked as if she'd just given him an early Christmas gift or offered to let him into her bed. Or maybe not that. He didn't really seem to be looking at her as if she were flesh and blood.

At least he wasn't looking at her the way Dylan usually did, with heat and frustration and wicked intent.

April picked up a copy of *Good Night, Moon* off the table and began to fan herself with it.

Dylan was looking at her that way again. As if he wanted to nibble his way down her body. Greg was launching into a discussion of the magazine article she'd confessed to reading.

And Jordie was chewing on his fist. Poor baby, he was hungry.

Hungry in a different way than Dylan apparently was. In fact, Greg appeared to be the least hungry person in the room, and he was the one she was supposed to be having lunch with.

Suddenly, April looked around at the three males she'd been sharing space with for the past two weeks. She would have so little time left with them. There were only so many kisses she would be allowed and then they would all be gone forever.

And she didn't just mean Jordie and Sam's kisses.

She was going to miss Dylan terribly once this job was over. As much as she'd fought against getting too close to him, walking away from him was going to leave an aching hole in her life.

And Jordie and Sam would grow up and she'd never even see a picture.

She looked at Greg, who was still talking, unaware that her mind had been wandering.

She glanced at Dylan, who was studying her from beneath his lashes, a glint of dark amber making her catch her breath. She wondered what he thought of Greg.

Was Greg the perfect mate for her? He was nice, but maybe she wasn't the world's greatest judge.

Maybe she needed another opinion.

Or three other opinions.

"I have an idea," she said suddenly, pulling Sam up onto her lap. "Let's all go out to lunch together."

Chapter Ten

"Isn't this nice?" April looked around at the family restaurant she had chosen. The butterflies in her stomach were having drag races. Of course, this wasn't the type of restaurant Greg had anticipated. He was a single man looking for a date with a single and very available woman.

And Dylan? She doubted he'd ever eaten in any establishment that had plastic salt shakers, but she couldn't have taken Sam and Jordie into a five-star restaurant. They would be lost and uncomfortable, and the management might be rude to them. Not that Dylan was likely to let that happen.

He smiled at her now, reassuringly, and she was reasonably certain that he had read the distress on her face.

"Good choice," he said, directing the hostess to seat them in an area with plenty of room for the boys.

"Yes, I'm sure the food here is acceptable," Greg said. He gave Dylan an appraising look as if the two men were in some sort of contest and he had just one-upped his opponent.

"April, why don't you sit there," Dylan said, taking Jordie from her and waiting for her to be seated. "I'll put the boys on either side of you, I'll sit next to Sam, since he likes a little more activity with his meal, and then Greg can sit opposite you. So that you can talk."

For a minute Greg looked like he was going to object as April was sandwiched between two babies in high chairs, but then he sat.

"It *does* make sense," she said soothingly. "We can maintain eye contact this way." Of course it probably would have made more sense if she hadn't asked Dylan and the boys to come along, but they were here and she was...well, actually she was glad to have them. Surrounded by the men she'd grown used to these past couple of weeks, she felt safe and happy.

"Why don't you and Greg talk for a moment while I get the boys some crackers to keep them content?" Dylan suggested.

"That sounds like a good idea," Greg said, hunching over the table toward April. "I want to talk to you about an article I read the other day. It was an old one, so you've probably already read it. It was written by Lila Guterman and appeared in the *Chronicle of Higher Education.* You know, it dealt with the theory that most mathematicians are past their prime at age thirty-five." His voice had started out low, but as Sam and Jordie were crumbling crackers and humming baby songs, his voice rose to a near shout toward the end.

April barely kept from smiling. "Yes, I know the one. One of the things she discusses is the fact that mathematics is one of the few fields where a person can do top-notch work without having a lot of experience."

"Yes, that's the one. You *have* read it," he said with apparent relief.

Perhaps he was thinking that she'd misrepresented herself online since she hadn't read any of the earlier articles he'd mentioned. A tiny prickle of resentment stirred in April. She shut it down. Hadn't she been the one to drag Dylan along because she wasn't sure she was safe with Greg?

"I've read it. I was especially interested in the part that dealt with the matter of life getting in the way of brilliance as a person gets older. Taking care of babies and such," she said, picking up a napkin and one of Jordie's cracker-and-saliva-encrusted hands and expertly wiping it clean.

He cooed as if to thank her. She kissed his almost clean hand.

When she glanced up, Greg was looking horrified. She wondered for a second if she'd misquoted the article, but then she saw him staring at Jordie's hand.

"He's a baby," she nearly said, barely stopping herself. Nevertheless she was sure she didn't quite hide her resentment.

"Come here, you," Dylan teased, starting to lift Jordie onto his lap, but she put her hand out and placed it on Dylan's.

"It's fine. Really," she said.

"Sorry, I don't have much experience with little ones," Greg said, and she sighed. Of course he didn't. What was wrong with her, expecting him to understand when she herself had been appalled at the prospect of this job two weeks ago?

"He's fine, but I'll take him for a few minutes," Dylan said.

She smiled her thanks and turned her attention back

to Greg, immersing herself in a discussion of Greg's latest mathematical research at the university where he taught.

When the food came, though, she automatically turned to help Jordie while Dylan helped Sam, and as if on cue, Greg turned to Dylan and asked him to discuss the problems inherent in the security systems of a research lab.

Dylan glanced at her out of the corner of his eye, and she simply smiled. Their exchange felt very private, somehow, even though they were seated in a group. Together they fed the boys while managing to eat a bit themselves. They took turns engaging in conversation with Greg.

He's intelligent, she thought. He's very nice, the kind of man most mothers would want their daughters to marry, the kind of man she should marry.

He doesn't make you burn to gaze into his eyes and press your body to his. The single thought invaded her mind. She quickly glanced toward Dylan as if he might have read her thoughts.

He was studying her intently, and she couldn't help wondering if that was the way he looked at a woman just before he eased her back onto the sheets and removed her clothes.

She jerked and tried to pretend that she was listening to what Greg was saying, but it was as if her mind and her body wouldn't let her tune out the man with the amber eyes.

A clanging sounded when Jordie sent his spoon clattering off the high chair and onto the table for the third time.

Automatically April leaned to pick up the piece of silverware, but when she reached out, her fingers brushed against Dylan's, who had gotten there first. She looked up and found he was staring at her, their hands entangled around the small bit of stainless steel.

Heat and longing rippled through her, and she opened her hand, relinquishing the spoon to him.

"Jordie, my man, we're going to have to learn to hold on to our utensils," Dylan said with a meaningful look at the little boy. "Can't be making our ladies work so hard."

"I think I can handle the weight of a spoon," she teased.

But it wasn't the spoon she couldn't handle. It was her reactions to Dylan that confused and disturbed her.

And Greg?

Oh my, she'd almost forgotten him. She turned to him now.

He was looking rather sad. "A penny for your thoughts," he said, and she blinked. Had he seen that exchange between her and Dylan? Guilt flowed through her. Greg was her guest. He was a very nice man, and he deserved to get what he'd come for. Her company.

"Can you watch the boys for the rest of the meal?" April asked Dylan softly, apologetically.

"Absolutely," he said. "Don't worry."

"I'm sorry, but I don't seem to be dividing my time very well," April admitted. "I suppose bringing them wasn't the best of ideas."

Dylan gave her a crooked smile. "Don't be sorry. The boys and I are fine. We can be happy just sitting here communing with each other. Come on, I'll move Jordie so that he and I can exchange long looks without peering around you. You just tend to your guest. Keep her occupied, Greg, will you?" he asked, quickly and efficiently rearranging the table and gathering the boys close to him.

April felt a small pang as the three of them moved farther away. She felt a bit cold, but resolutely she turned herself to Greg, who was looking slightly relieved.

For the next forty minutes, she devoted herself to eating and making conversation with the man she'd once termed "the perfect mate" for her. He was intelligent, he was friendly, and she realized with a bit of distress that no matter how hard she tried, she couldn't give him her complete attention. A part of her was sitting on the other side of the table, smiling into Dylan's eyes, watching as he slipped a spoon into Sam's little lips to give him some soup.

A very large part of her was aware that while Dylan was taking care of the boys, he was watching over her as well. He kept an eye on Greg from time to time as if waiting for the man to jump her and drag her down onto the carpeted floor.

It was a silly thought. Greg's eyes only lit up when she invited him to discuss his work. Then his hands flew and he smiled, his words rushed on. She had the feeling that she could get up and place a mannequin in her chair and he would not know the difference. As long as the mannequin could discuss the latest scientific and math journals.

"You're a wonderful listener," Greg said suddenly, startling her, and he leaned closer, halfway over the table. He reached out. For her hand?

A dinner roll came out of left field and slid between them.

"Sam, behave yourself," Dylan said in a teasing voice, levering himself between them to retrieve the roll. "Sorry," he said to Greg.

April knew it wouldn't be smart to look at him, but she couldn't help it. When she glanced up, he winked at her and smiled. She smiled back, and for a second she thought that he was going to shove Greg out of the way, lean across the table himself and kiss her.

If he did that, what would she do?

She was very afraid that she would kiss him back.

"No problem," Greg said, but he sat back in his chair as Dylan regained his own place at the table.

A clatter at the next table brought everyone's attention around. A man jumped up, complaining about the time, and soon everyone in the room was pulling out watches.

"Damn, he's right, it's getting late and I have to go," Greg said. "But it looks like the boys aren't done eating yet. Good thing we came in separate cars. Valentine, would you mind if I take April home, and you can meet her back there later?" he asked, standing up.

"Oh, no, that wouldn't be fair to Dylan," April said, panic assailing her as she started to rise.

"It's fine, April. Don't worry. He came to see you. Go say goodbye to the man," Dylan said, and his eyes were dark and unwavering when she looked at him.

He knew. He knew that she was attracted to him while she was supposed to be entertaining Greg, and he knew just as she did that it wouldn't fly. Greg was the type of man she'd been looking for, the kind she needed.

Stiffly, she nodded her thanks and followed Greg out of the restaurant. She turned once to blow kisses at the boys. Like a mom, she thought, then panicked and forced the thought away.

Greg didn't seem the type to want kids, but then lots of men didn't. Dylan didn't. He didn't want genuine closeness. He just wanted to touch her.

And heaven help her, she wanted to touch him, too.

It was the last thought she allowed herself before she followed Greg out into the parking lot.

* * *

Dylan paced the floor, watching the clock hands circle.

"Where is she?" he asked himself, but of course he knew where she was. She was with Greg, a very nice man, the perfect man that she'd been waiting for. Greg, who liked the fact that she was a good listener.

Greg, who no doubt liked her for a lot more than that. He was, after all, a man.

"And he's the man she wants," Dylan reminded himself, "so don't even bother threatening him if he touches her. Unless she doesn't want him to touch her, that is."

And there was the rub. April wanted things, things she could get from a man like Greg, and soon she was going to get them. It was obvious that Greg was the man for her. He knew his science, he knew his math, he was nonthreatening, he wouldn't get her pregnant and then leave her. No, if a man like Greg conceived a child, he would marry the woman even if he didn't want children.

He was the right kind of man.

And that was the killer, Dylan thought, because he should be happy for April for finding what she wanted so badly. Greg would make her smile.

She had a lovely smile.

Soon all he would have of that smile would be memories. And pictures, he added. He intended to take pictures. Lots of them before she and the boys left here.

The sound of a car door slamming brought him to his feet. He moved to the door, opened it.

There she was, and there was that smile.

"You had a good time," he said simply.

She shrugged. "Greg was very nice," she agreed.

"The perfect man."

"I suppose some would say that."

"Do you think... Do you plan to marry him?"

"We've only just met."

"He likes you. He wants you."

She grinned. "Not like that."

"Exactly like that. I saw him before we left for lunch. He was staring at your legs."

"How do you know?"

"Because *I* was staring at your legs." He gazed down into her eyes, looking for something, some hint that she was newly in love. But he couldn't read her wary expression. Her gaze dropped to his lips. Then she lowered her head.

"He's a nice man," she repeated.

"I agree, and I wasn't criticizing." Even though a stubborn part of him wished he could. "I'm sorry if it sounded that way," he said, and he gathered her into his arms.

She met his gaze. Those violet eyes of hers were so open, so uncertain. She trembled as he watched her. Finally she took a deep breath.

"Thank you for watching the boys," she whispered. "Where are they?"

"Asleep. I tucked them in thirty minutes ago."

For a second she looked crestfallen. "I missed it."

He grinned and tucked one finger beneath her chin. "You'll be there tomorrow."

But not for too many tomorrows. They both knew that.

"I don't think Greg was looking at my legs," she finally said, stubbornly. "Not unless I had quadratic equations written on them."

Dylan grinned. He stepped back and looked down at her beautiful legs. He placed his hand on her hip and curled his fingers, bunching the soft yellow material of her skirt, pulling it so that it climbed higher on her thighs. "I don't see any equations," he whispered. "Just beautiful skin. Just you."

"I can't believe you're doing that," she whispered, but she didn't stop him.

"It's because I'm not the perfect man. I couldn't look at your legs and discuss mathematics." He tugged and the material slid higher.

"Greg wasn't looking at my legs. You made that up."

"He's a man, April. I watched him all through lunch. He wants you. What man wouldn't?"

She gazed up at him, wide-eyed, much too innocent. "Lots of men wouldn't," she said with a straight face. She really believed that. And she trusted him. Heavens, but she trusted him.

His lips hovered over hers. If he leaned just a breath closer, he could touch her, kiss her, feel her body against his.

And she would respond. She wasn't immune to him. Her breathing was broken, shallow. For a second he thought he heard her whisper a quadratic equation.

He leaned closer to her lips, gazed into those trusting violet eyes. And he realized she'd been here before. Trusting a man who would hurt her. A less-than-perfect man.

There was no getting around the ugly truth. Slowly, Dylan forced himself to ease away from April. He let go of her dress. The cloth slid down her legs and back into place. He stroked his fingers down her cheek.

"Go to sleep, April," he whispered as he let her go.

"I'm not a child, Dylan."

He shook his head. "If you stay, I'm going to kiss you. And if I kiss you, I'll definitely want you in my bed before the night is over. You see, I'm not as nice as Greg. I'm never going to be the perfect man that he is. If you came to me and told me that you wanted me, I'd take you.''

"For a night," she said.

"Yes," he agreed.

He expected her to look crestfallen, but the look in her eyes was speculative. She licked her lips.

"Might be worth it," she whispered.

It was all he could do to stop himself from grabbing her, bending her over his arm and kissing his way madly down her throat, slipping the buttons open on that prim yellow dress and flicking open the catch on her bra that hid her enticing curves from his view.

Only the fact that there was a tomorrow stopped him. And tomorrow she would cry. She'd remember her mother and her grandmother and that guy who left her before, and she'd know that once again, a man had had his way with her with no thought to the consequences.

"Go to sleep," he urged her. "I'm going out for a while."

She blinked. He knew she wanted to ask where.

It would have done her no good. He didn't know where. He just knew that if he stayed here, he might set wheels in motion that should never have been turned.

"Sleep tight," he said and slipped out the door.

For hours he drove, thinking of April wiping Jordie's hand and kissing it, slipping raspberries into Sam's mouth, curling up on her bed at night, scribbling in the boys' journals.

He wanted her, but he wasn't alone.

At least three men wanted her. Greg, of course, and himself.

But there was the third man, the one who had followed her, maybe the one who had hung up the phone earlier today.

Jason Olney wanted her, too.

And now was the time to let him know once and for all he couldn't ever have her.

It wasn't the best of plans, it wasn't the best of hours to do this, but pent-up energy and frustration suffused his body, and he had to get rid of it somehow.

Jason Olney would serve as the perfect target to vent his frustrations.

Chapter Eleven

Well, at least the man was still up. Dylan noted that the lights were still on in Jason Olney's lush Lake Shore Drive brownstone. He was probably plotting how to terrorize another woman—or how to punish April some more for daring to refuse to date him.

"The day she dates offal like you, Olney, is the day I become a monk."

Dylan allowed cold rage to slide through his veins, crystallizing his intent. He quickly mounted the stairs and rang the doorbell.

A woman opened the door, a somewhat frumpy though expensively clad woman. She looked as if life had slapped her around a few times. His investigation these past few days told him that it had.

Dylan smiled politely. "Excuse me. Mrs. Olney?"

She stared at him warily. "We don't allow solicitors." She pointed to a sign on the door.

"I'm not a solicitor, ma'am. My name is Dylan Valentine. I'm a business associate of your husband."

She bit her lip. "I don't remember hearing your name."

Dylan smiled again, wondering if it was worth the trouble to reassure this woman. She looked as if she'd learned to be suspicious of everyone and everything in life.

"It's a very recent association, but I'm afraid that something's come up and he and I have some rather urgent business to attend to, something that may affect the future of his firm. May I come in?"

She hesitated. He hated to put her in this position. No telling what a man like Olney would do to a wife if he were upset.

"I won't keep him long, and I'll explain that I insisted on seeing him," he said gently. "Believe me, I have news that he'll want to hear immediately."

Reluctantly, she opened the door farther and motioned him in. Leading him through the house, she knocked softly on a door.

"He's in his office," she explained.

When the door opened and Jason was standing there, she quickly stepped back. "Someone to see you," she said, withdrawing back into the hallway.

"What the hell?" Olney spluttered.

Dylan didn't wait for Olney to get his wits about him. He simply stepped forward, causing Olney to step back. The door fell shut with a whispering click.

"What are you doing here, Valentine? You must have lied to my wife to talk your way in here."

Dylan smiled slightly. Now came the good part. "On the contrary, Olney. Everything I told her was the truth."

"And what was that?" He crossed his arms and moved into Dylan's space, trying to bar him from com-

ing any farther into the room. No wonder, Dylan
thought. His personal phone book was open on the desk.

"Late-night calls?" Dylan asked, slipping easily past
the man and perching on the desk. "Ah, I see, lots of
ladies in here. How does your wife feel about that?"

"Those women are all business associates. Not that
it's any of your business."

"Not that it is, but I seem to recall being told that
you were dating a teacher at the high school. Mind if I
look more closely?"

"Don't touch that." Jason muscled his way in and
slammed the book closed.

Dylan raised one brow. He smiled. "Doesn't matter,
you know. People like to talk, and I've heard enough in
the past two days to convince myself that you're slime.
Not that there was any question of that."

"Get out of my office, Valentine. I'm calling the po-
lice."

Shaking his head, Dylan shrugged. "You could do
that, but I doubt that they'll be interested. After all, I
have a legitimate business reason for being here, and I
didn't force my way into your house."

"Legitimate business reason. What the hell are you
talking about?"

"Not much. Just that your partners and I have had a
chat. After hearing some of the things you've been up
to, they're not exactly sure they can trust a man who
cheats on so many levels. We've made a business deal.
I'll secure both of their offices and they'll keep their
heads turned and their ears closed any time you and I
might need to have a chat."

"That's ridiculous. I've worked with both of them for
years."

"True, but I understand that they're both considering

breaking ties with you. You haven't made many friends in the business, have you, Olney?''

"What are you really here for, Valentine?"

Dylan shrugged. "Just a little justice. A friendly warning, if you will."

"You can't threaten me. I know the law. I know my rights."

"I'm sure you do, but the thing is, Olney, I just don't give a damn. You haven't done anything that's, technically speaking, illegal, but you've done a few things that just might tick a few people off. I happen to know a few of those people."

"I've achieved great things in the courtroom."

"I'm not talking about the courtroom. I'm talking about your private life. If you're going to keep clients coming to you, Jason, you're just going to have to have an epiphany tonight. You'll have to agree to walk the straight and narrow. I've had my investigators checking you out for the past few days, and you've been pretty messy in some respects. That's not good. You've hurt people. And, in this case, you've tried to hurt the wrong person, so…what can I do, Olney? You've pretty much shoved me into a corner. I'm afraid I just can't approve of the way you've been conducting yourself. So, if I hear even one hint of you harassing another woman, following another woman or calling another woman that isn't either strictly business or your wife, I'm just going to have to react, pull some strings, make some phone calls. Sometimes it's a good thing knowing people in the media. Know what I mean, Olney?"

Jason shook his head vigorously, his eyes rolling around in his head. "Are you threatening me, Valentine?"

Dylan clucked his tongue and shook his head.

"Threaten is such an ugly word, isn't it? Let's just say that I stand for truth and justice. You know, like those guys in the comic books. Kind of hokey, but there you have it."

"This is about that witch, April, isn't it?"

Dylan really didn't want to react. He didn't want to rise to the bait, not when he was making Olney sweat, but some things a man just couldn't ignore. He leaned forward over the desk and got into Olney's face. "If you're referring to April Pruitt, I have several suggestions for you. Don't ever mention her name again. Don't call her. Don't try to see her. And if any other young innocent should come your way, that rule goes for her as well. I don't interfere in what happens between a man and his wife, but I can't abide those who use money or power or physical intimidation to threaten others, especially women or children. Do I make myself clear, Olney?"

For several seconds, Jason Olney just stood there glaring at Dylan.

"What's the deal here? What are you planning? What's in it for me if I cooperate?"

"Simple. I'll leave you alone to attend to your business."

"And if I don't you'll—"

"I'll make it a point to crush you. I happen to know that while you make a tidy sum of money, you also like to live a bit above your means. Could be uncomfortable if someone should cut off the flow of incoming cash."

"I don't believe you can do that."

"Jason, Jason, Jason, be smart. In your line of work, image is so important, and you've been, well, you've been a bit indiscreet at times, a bit lazy in covering your tracks. Last year you were, um, dating a Ms. Baker, weren't you? Her father, a very influential man in the business community didn't know about it, did he? If he did, I'm sure that he didn't know that you were a married man. I understand that he recently was persuaded to throw his business to your firm. I'm afraid he might be shocked if he knew that you had once slept with his daughter. I understand that he's very protective of Bridget.''

''You don't know him.''

At that, Dylan sighed. ''Ah, Jason, I know so many people. The Valentines are an old family in the area, and security is such a big business. But, if you really don't care?'' He reached for the phone, set it to speakerphone and punched in some numbers.

''His business number,'' Dylan whispered, ''but then you knew that.''

When the phone began to ring, Jason stepped forward and cut the connection.

''Well, that was a shame. I'm sure he has caller identification. He'll probably wonder why you called him at…'' Dylan looked at his watch. ''Eleven-thirty at night.''

''All right, you could cost me some of my business. You've made your point.''

''You'd better hope that I have,'' Dylan said. ''From now on, I think it would be best if you remained a faithful, loving husband. If your marriage is unhappy, then end it before you begin dating, but for heaven's sake, keep your nose clean, if you can.''

''I'm not an idiot.''

Dylan smiled condescendingly. ''No, you're a bully. That ends here.''

''This is blackmail.''

''It's just good business, the only kind I do.'' He

moved toward the door. No point in sticking around longer.

"I hope you and the witch are happy."

Dylan knew he should have simply walked out, but this was April that Olney was talking about. And it irked Dylan tremendously that he and April could never find happiness together. It just wasn't in the cards.

He couldn't have her any more than this worm could.

"That's Ms. Pruitt to you, Olney, and for the record, she's much too good for you."

Of course she was much too good for *him,* too, Dylan thought as he left. But he'd never made the mistake that Olney had. He'd never thought he could have her.

He couldn't, but he could protect her, and he could do his best to make sure she got the happiness she was looking for.

In just three days she would leave Dylan's house and his world behind, April thought four days later. It was probably a good thing. She was growing too comfortable here, something she had to guard against.

Last night Dylan had even taken her to meet his friends Spencer and Ethan. She'd liked them immediately because they so obviously cared for Dylan. And she'd felt comfortable since they were all there to help Ethan's employee, Maggie, whom he'd also hired at the auction. Maggie was in Cinderella training and she'd needed an audience. April and Kate—Spencer's find from the auction—had provided the necessary feminine perspective. Dylan had laughed a lot. He'd been at ease with these friends, the only people she knew of that he allowed close.

But the evening had ended early, and one more day had ticked off the calendar. The rest would pass quickly.

She was very aware of it, and apparently, Dylan was, too, since he spent a lot of time taking pictures of her and the boys. Or sometimes of just her alone.

"I want Viv to have a record," he said noncommittally when she asked why. But he looked a little sheepish when he said it. She wondered if he would keep at least one photo for himself or would he simply want to forget this time?

For her part, April did her best to make the days memorable. She and Dylan took the boys to the children's museum and let them press all the buttons. She read rulebooks of games and tried to play as many of them as she could with the boys, and she always did her best to get Dylan to join in. Sometimes he did, but often he would shake his head. She knew getting involved wasn't easy for him. Too risky. Relationships demanded too much.

Still, when she needed his help, he never turned her down. Which was good, since she was going to need him for the project she had in mind for after dinner tonight.

"Come on," she whispered conspiratorially. "We're going to make a playhouse for the boys."

He raised one brow. "A-pril," he drawled. "Have you been holding out on me? Do you have carpentry skills that I'm unaware of?"

She wrinkled her nose. "Not a real, build-it kind of playhouse. A temporary one. Made out of furniture and blankets and that kind of thing. I called Agnes Mason and she told me that every kid she's ever met has loved crawling around in makeshift houses. It makes them feel safe and protected, and 'it's very important for toddlers to know that they are in a secure environment,'" she quoted, holding out one of the baby manuals she'd started to accumulate.

"You've amassed quite a library, lady," Dylan said softly. "You're billing that stuff to me, aren't you?"

She only hesitated for a second. "I can use these in my work."

"You teach high school."

"But what if one of my students gets pregnant?" she asked.

Dylan had to admire her inventiveness. "That was good, April. You were very fast with that response. Have you ever had a pregnant student?"

"No," she admitted, "but it happens. It might."

He started to argue and insist that she charge him for the books. These were his brothers, after all, but maybe she wanted to take the manuals with her for when she had her own children. If he paid for them, he knew there was no way she would feel free to do that.

"We'll talk about it later," he decided. "Now how do we go about building this house?"

She smiled up at him through her lashes. "Well, I think we rearrange the furniture, put some chairs in here and there as supports, use the cushions from the sofas as walls or even ceilings in places, and set up a kind of a maze. Then we fasten a sheet over the top like a canopy and let them crawl around inside their makeshift tent. I'm told by colleagues that their kids loved this kind of thing when they were young. Unfortunately I couldn't find anything about such things online. No step-by-step instructions and definitely no pictures."

Dylan smiled at the note of chagrin in her voice. Of course, *he* knew what she was talking about. He'd just been teasing her earlier.

"You never made a playhouse when you were a kid?"

"Oh, no, my mother wouldn't have gone for that. Too messy and disruptive."

He was beginning to wonder if April's mother had allowed her to have any fun at all. It seemed as if she spent a lot of time trying to make sure that April wasn't too messy, too disruptive, too emotional or too passionate. Dylan raised one brow at that last thought. He thanked the heavens that her mother hadn't been able to nag the passion out of her. April might want to deny her nature, but there were some things that just couldn't be hidden.

"I think we can figure this out without diagrams," he said gently. "I spent a lot of time on my own as a kid. Building places where I could hide away was one of my favorite activities. Of course, I didn't have anyone to help me. This will be a new experience."

"You know how?" she asked, her eyes widening with apparent anticipation. "This could be fun. Exciting."

He looked down at her parted lips. "Definitely exciting."

"Where do we start?" she asked.

By kissing those berry-pink lips, he wanted to say, but he shook his head to clear it. "We'll use the sofa as a starting place, then build from there."

"It sounds like a plan."

A much safer plan than dragging April into his arms and sliding to the ground with her would be, he agreed.

For the next few minutes, they arranged and rearranged furniture, making sure that there were no sharp corners to trip the boys up and plenty of little exits and entrances. When they had everything arranged to their satisfaction, April found a large sheet, and she and Dylan fastened the corners to the backs of four chairs.

"What do you think?" she asked, gazing at their handiwork.

"Well..."

"I know, I know, it's just a bunch of furniture topped by a sheet, but you know how Sam and Jordie are. They'll love crawling around inside and pretending that they're really doing something adventurous. They'll probably drag all their toys inside and set up house. Of course, we'll have to supervise them closely and make sure they're safe at all times. I hope we left them enough room to maneuver easily and that the entrances are clearly visible from anywhere inside. I wouldn't want them to get scared." She frowned slightly.

"Only one way to find out if it's right," Dylan offered.

She grinned up at him. "I was hoping you'd say that."

She was so transparent, more eager than a kid, actually.

"Shall we try it?" he asked.

"Let's. You start on one side and I'll start on another. I'll meet you in the middle." And she dropped to her knees and started to crawl inside. For one delicious second, he was treated to a vision of her luscious backside, and he was half tempted to crawl in right behind her.

But that wasn't the plan, was it? This was about checking out the house for the boys. So, moving around the perimeter of the makeshift playhouse, Dylan entered on the opposite side.

Cushions from the sofas throughout the house had been raided, providing low walls set far enough apart to give the boys plenty of room to maneuver. The airy light blue sheet hung just above his head, providing a safe, comforting ceiling.

From this vantage point, he was enclosed in a soft cocoon, the world far away. And April was moving toward him on her hands and knees, encased in this silent world with him.

She crawled right in under his nose and looked up from beneath her lashes, her violet eyes sparkling.

"What do you think?" she whispered.

He thought she was too close, that he shouldn't allow himself to be alone with her.

"Do you think they'll like it?" She probed. "Do *you* like it?"

He barely stifled a groan. "I like it," he managed to say.

He'd thought that he'd successfully concealed the desire that was coursing through him, but apparently he was wrong. She looked up through her lashes.

"It's very…private, isn't it?"

"Very."

"Perhaps this wasn't such a good idea."

"No doubt it was a very bad idea."

"You know I do my best not to give in to my emotions and my—my—"

"Passions," he suggested, swallowing thickly.

She wet her lips. "Yes," she said, her voice faint. "My passions. My mother always told me that my passion would be my downfall."

And suddenly Dylan was angry. "Your passion is your beauty," he said, and then he sat back on his heels and reached out. His hands grasped her waist and he reeled her in, pulling her up against him.

And then he couldn't wait any longer to taste her. He dipped his head and brought his lips down on hers.

She melted against him. She flowed into his arms, and her lips moved beneath his own. Her eyes fluttered closed and her scent filled his world.

"I shouldn't be doing this," she whispered softly, when he had pulled back to give her air.

He kissed her eyelids, her cheeks, the curve of her jaw.

"You shouldn't," he agreed, "but not because you should deny your passionate nature. It's a lovely nature, it's what makes you you."

"But what if I can't control it?" She burrowed closer and her lips nipped at his throat.

He was barely controlling himself. He was dying to lay her down, flick open the buttons on her clothing and bare every inch of her to his view.

"I'll control it," he said, thickly, and he didn't know if he was trying to convince himself or her.

"That's not the way it works." She shifted in his arms and her soft breasts pressed against him. He hadn't thought he could grow any harder, but he'd been wrong.

A low groan rumbled through him.

She was right. That wasn't the way it worked. She had to live with herself in the morning, and if she thought she'd given herself to a man who would hurt her, she'd think she'd failed.

Dylan took a deep breath. He kissed her again, gently, this time. He grasped her forearms and pulled back, gazing down into her eyes.

"I'm not going to deny that I want you so badly that I'm not exactly thinking straight," he said, "but I know this much is true. You're a passionate woman who feels things deeply, and that's a wonderful thing. The perfect man won't want you to deny him all that you are and all that you can offer. With him, it will be wonderful. I think your mother was wrong about you. You're not too emotional. You just need the right person to give that great gift to.''

She looked up into his eyes and smiled sadly. She framed his face with her palms and leaned forward, giving him a soft kiss on the lips.

He lost it then and pulled her in to him. He touched her with his lips, his hands sliding down her body, cupping her breasts.

''Just this one moment,'' he whispered.

''Yes, just one moment,'' she agreed, and she twined herself about him. She offered up her mouth for another kiss.

Feasting on her lips, he knew this one moment wouldn't be enough.

But after he'd kissed her seven or eight times, after he'd tunneled his fingers through her hair, after she'd twined herself about him and fire had leapt between them, he somehow managed to pull back.

Only concern for her could have made him do that.

He needed to tone things down, take them to a safer plane. If he hurt her, he'd be far worse than Jason Olney. Because she had trusted him.

''I think,'' he began, somehow dredging up a quirky grin, ''this is one great playhouse.''

It was the right thing to do.

She laughed shakily. ''Definitely has possibilities,'' she agreed.

''When the boys wake up, they'll be delighted. I'll tell them it was all your idea,'' he said.

''I'll tell them that you were the architect and the engineer.''

''They're going to have so much fun,'' he promised. ''They'll remember you forever.'' Because he knew that she was starting to worry about the fact that she would never see Jordie and Sam again, and he couldn't promise that she would. If she saw Jordie and Sam, she would see *him* as well, and that just wouldn't be right. For either of them.

"I hope they at least remember that a lady once came and loved her time with them," she said softly.

But at that moment, the doorbell rang.

April looked confused. "Were you expecting someone?" It was nearly midnight.

Dylan shook his head. Damn it, it was probably Olney come to cause problems. "No one," he said tersely. "Don't worry. Stay here. I'll take care of it."

Quickly he extricated himself from the playhouse. His last thought before he opened the door was that April was coming up behind him. He moved to block her from view. Olney wasn't going to get a chance to aim a barb at her.

But when the door opened wide, he blinked.

"Dylan, I couldn't wait." The woman launched herself through the door into his arms.

"Viv?"

"Where are they? I couldn't wait. The marriage is off, and I want my boys. I've come to take them home. Tonight."

Chapter Twelve

The house was so silent that she could hear it breathing, April thought an hour later after the boys had gone home with their mother. Awakened from their sleep, they'd blinked and tried to smile and then had yawned as April and Dylan and Vivian had packed them up.

"They were good. They were very good," Dylan had said, awkwardly patting the boys on the back as Vivian had hugged them close, and April wondered which relatives had told stories on him when his mother had come to get him. She wondered if his mother had withheld affection as a result of those bad reports.

Everything had happened in such a whirl. Vivian was clearly upset by what had happened or not happened with her former fiancé and she wanted to be on her way.

"It'll be fine. I'm sure it'll be fine. He wasn't right for me. He really didn't want children. How could he not want them?" she said, hugging her babies close.

Exactly, April wanted to say. How could he not want those babies? But she couldn't, because Dylan didn't want babies, and she didn't blame him a bit. There were special circumstances. Maybe Viv's fiancé had had similar circumstances.

Still, everything just flew by, and suddenly Viv was ready to take the drowsy little boys out the door.

"Oh. Wait," April cried. "Wait, please. I have something." And she ran up the stairs and into the study. Tossing things around, she grabbed a big envelope and stuffed in all of the pictures that she and Dylan had taken. She grabbed the boys' journals off the desk.

"It's all here," she said as she flew down the stairs. "A record of their time here, so you won't miss any of the special moments. They're so beautiful." And her voice broke. She knew that she was near tears and she quickly moved forward and touched her lips to each soft little cheek. She breathed in their scents and dared to stroke their hair just one more time. "You have a wonderful life," she whispered to Sam. "Don't break too many girls' hearts. And you don't be afraid to speak up when you want some attention," she told Jordie. "Goodbye."

Dylan watched her, his amber eyes intense. She was sure he hadn't missed the trace of tears in her eyes or in her voice.

But she was more worried about him than about herself. She moved up beside him. "Don't let them go like this," she whispered. "It's okay to let them know you'll miss them, and I know you will."

He turned to her, he opened his mouth. For a minute she thought he was going to deny what he was feeling, that he was going to tell her that this was none of her business.

But then he nodded tersely, one quick, jerky movement.

"May I?" he asked Vivian stiffly, and he held out his hands.

She smiled. "Of course. You're their brothers." And she forked over Sam.

Dylan took the little boy into his big hands and held him up at eye level. "You're something special, you know. You make sure and keep your mom and your brother laughing, okay?" And he brought Sam down close and hugged him, then kissed him before turning him back over to Viv.

Then she passed Jordie to him, and he pulled Jordie in close. He kissed the top of the baby's head. "You speak up for yourself, okay?" he whispered near the tiny curve of his ear. "And if any bullies start bothering you just because you're quiet, you just give me a call. I'll be there right away."

April didn't remember much after that. The tears were coursing down her cheeks. She knew that she said good-bye to Viv and thanked her for letting the boys stay with her and Dylan. She remembered calling goodbye a hundred times and throwing as many kisses.

And now the boys were gone.

She and Dylan were alone.

And her reason for being here had just driven away.

She stared up at the man she knew she loved with anguish in her heart and the fiercest determination to hide it. He'd been hurt so many times in his life. How could she hurt him again by loving him and making him feel like half a man when he had to admit that he could never return that love?

"These last weeks were fun, weren't they?" she said.

"They were...something," he agreed, and he traced her cheek with his fingertip. She knew he was following the tracks of her tears.

She bit her lip, knowing what she had to do next. "I think I'll go pack now," she said.

He sucked in a visible breath. His finger trembled slightly and he pulled away, shoving his hand into his pocket. "You don't have to leave tonight. Tomorrow will be fine."

But that wasn't true. If she stayed the night without the boys here as an excuse, she would die a million deaths, knowing he was so close and yet untouchable. Her reason for being here was gone, and now she had to go. If she stayed, she would want so much. She would suffer, and so would he, because he would know that she was suffering. She was sure that she couldn't hide a love this big now that she knew it existed.

April shook her head. "I think… I think I want to go now. Lots of things to do this summer before school begins. And it wouldn't be a good idea for me to stay. When you and I are alone together…well, bad things happen."

He looked as if she had struck him. Of course, she meant good things, wonderful things, insanely seductive and powerfully moving things.

"If I stayed, Dylan," she said, wanting to explain, "we know where I'd end up and that it would be a mistake. A wonderful mistake, but still a mistake. There's no future for us. But I do want you to know one thing," she said. "You have my gratitude for hiring me for this job. I didn't want it at first, but I'm very glad I took it. Because of the boys, but also because of you. I think your relatives missed out on so much, not getting to know you. It was their loss and your parents' loss. They'll never know that, but it's true."

He stood silently by her side for a long moment. He probably didn't believe her words, and she felt sad for that. He stared down at her, and she felt his presence like a powerful magnet. Just one step and she could be in his arms. Just one "yes" and she could have what she wanted so badly. But she could only have it one time, and that one time would be enough to haunt her forever. Better never to know what she would miss.

"I'll bring your car around," he finally said.

They went their separate ways. Her packing didn't take long, since she didn't put much thought into it. Just mechanically threw things into her bags. In no time, it seemed, she'd removed every trace of herself from Dylan's house.

All except one thing.

She came to him, a suitcase in one hand, the package in another. She held it out.

Dylan frowned. "A gift?"

She shrugged. "A beginning. For you and the boys."

He stared down into her eyes for long seconds, studying her. Then he nodded. He unwrapped the package carefully. He peeled back the green-and-blue paper. Reverently, he picked up the train engine.

She twisted her fingers together nervously. "You can learn woodworking together someday," she said, knowing that someday wouldn't include her. "You can build on to it. You can go back...with them," she added, and her voice broke.

April looked up through a mist and saw the wonder in Dylan's eyes. "You wanted me to have my childhood back," he said softly, "but you've given me so much more. You know that, don't you? This gives me a reason to keep the boys coming back for years. Thank you."

She shook her head. "I know it's not the same as if it had happened when you were young."

His eyes were dark, so dark.

"It's better. It's from you." And he crushed her to him once in a hard, quick kiss. Then he pulled back. "You'd better go. Quickly. I'll follow you home."

"There's no need."

"There's every need. April, please. Let me." In another world, another time, his words might have been said as he made love to her, as he offered to remove her clothing, as he took her body in his hands and lowered his lips to her skin to offer her a taste of shattering paradise.

She closed her eyes.

"April?"

She nodded once, hard, then climbed into her car.

The drive was forever. She could sense Dylan behind her. She was so aware that once she reached her house, he would drive away from her for all time.

But when she got to her house, he stepped from his car. She didn't have to ask why. He was going to see her safely into her house.

Fumbling for the keys, she wanted to get the door open faster—to end this torture. She wanted it to open more slowly—to keep Dylan at her side for one more second.

It didn't matter. Long or short, the door was opened. She turned to Dylan.

"Don't say it. Don't say anything," he whispered. "Just do this once more."

He kissed her. Softly, sweetly, his lips moving over her own. Gently, caressingly, with warmth and regret and goodbye.

"Have a perfect life, sweetheart," he said. "And April, don't worry about Jason. I want you to know that he won't be bothering you anymore. I don't want you to have to live with that fear."

She opened her mouth to ask what he meant, but he shook his head.

"It's nothing dramatic. I just pulled some business strings. Now go inside, sweetheart, so I'll know you're safe once I'm gone."

Numbly, she nodded. She took a silent step backward, and he closed the door. Moving to the window in the dark, she watched him drive away to a home she no longer had a right to enter.

He was gone. Her perfect man.

He'd always liked his solitude, so why was he cursing it so much now when he'd only regained it last night? Dylan asked himself. Not that he didn't know.

His distress wasn't from the loss of the boys, though he missed them. The boys he would see again. Viv would be happy to encourage a bit of closeness between him and his brothers, and this time he meant to take her up on her offer.

So no, it wasn't the boys.

The truth was, he was missing the clack of April's computer keys, the way she liked to spout little irrelevant but charming facts, the way her eyes lit up when she played a game with the boys for the first time and ended up being enchanted herself. Let's face it, he just plain missed everything that she was. With an ache so deep that it was almost physical. He felt like half of his soul had just walked away.

"Too bad. You can't have her. Deal with it."

He couldn't. He had returned to this empty house last night and realized he'd lost the gift for solitude. Solitude might have served him well in the past, but it was no substitute for the woman you loved.

He loved April.

And there was not a thing he could do about it. Because she was looking for her perfect man. He knew darn well what she wanted, exactly what she wanted. And he wasn't it.

So change. You want something badly enough, you can change.

It wasn't the first time that thought had occurred to him. As a child, his relatives had told him often enough that he could change and become what they wanted him to be.

Although most often they just wanted him to be gone. For the first time in his life, Dylan smiled at that.

April thought that his relatives and his parents had missed out when they'd passed up the chance to get to know him.

His smile grew broader.

What a woman. What an amazing gift of a woman. A man might risk anything, he might *do* anything, even something incredibly crazy for a woman like April.

April frowned at her computer screen. She'd been gone from Dylan's house for one day, she'd only been there two-and-a-half weeks, and now she was a complete mess.

Her mother would be shaking her head. "You're just like your grandmother," she would say. And what did that mean?

Dylan said that she wasn't too emotional, she wasn't too passionate. So why was she so miserable now? Why was she moping just like she'd seen her grandmother mope?

Love could be devastating if a man didn't love you back.

"And what if he did?" she asked herself. For a moment she thought about what it would be like if Dylan loved her, if they had their own babies. She pictured him with two toddlers, his dark hair mussed from playing games with the babies—or mussed because she'd threaded her fingers through the silky strands while they'd been making love.

The image made her gasp, startled her out of her daydream and back into reality. Dylan thought she should nurture her passion with the right man. The right man could satisfy her desire *and* make her happy.

How could she explain that *he* made her happy? So it looked like happiness and passion weren't in the cards for her. They were right out the window.

And life had to go on. Somehow. Somehow she had to find solace, balance, at least contentment.

But maybe that wasn't possible. She needed to know that it was, to hear how it could be, that there could be contentment in her life even if there wasn't a grand passion.

Quickly she reached for the phone and dialed her mother's number.

"April?" her mother asked when she picked up the phone. "What's wrong? You sound like you've been crying. What's happened, baby? Tell Mom."

She wanted to. She wanted to go crawling to her mother and spill out her tears, like she'd done the last time, but something stopped her. An image of Dylan filled her mind. To discuss him would be to betray him. He'd promised her nothing, he was in no way at fault for how she was feeling. And besides, that wasn't why she'd called.

"I'm fine, Mom, just a little summer blues. You know how it is when you're a teacher and you're temporarily faced with a lot of free time on your hands. I didn't call to tell you I had problems, Mom. I called to ask you something."

"Well, that's good then. That's what I'm here for. Ask away."

"I've been thinking about our family lately, and I just wanted to know, was Grandma happy? In the end, when she'd lived so many years, do you think she was happy?"

Her mother snorted over the wires. "Who knows? You know how she was. Always reaching for the stars. Could anyone be happy like that?"

Her mother couldn't, but...

"But did she say anything? Anything at all about how her life had played out."

She could almost hear her mother's deep shrug. "Once she said, 'Marlene, lots of it was fun.' Your grandfather was a very special man, and then when he was gone, there was more. She said that I wouldn't understand. That I'd only remember the bad things. She told me that if I would concentrate on getting past the bad things in life and reaching out for the best, I would be happier. She always thought I settled for second best. I never seemed to make her happy."

April blinked at that. It was what she'd thought about her own mother many times, that she could never really seem to make her proud or happy.

"Mom, were you and Dad happy?"

"Of course we were." Her mother's voice was indignant.

"No, I mean really, really happy. Did you feel joy when you saw him?"

"Joy is highly overrated. Your father and I had a good marriage."

"Didn't you ever feel that way about any man?"

There was a long silence. "If I did, I got over it, and I learned from it, and I was satisfied with your father."

For a second April tried to imagine her mother's eyes lighting up as a man came into the room. It was impossible, especially when she'd spent her whole life watching her mother fuss at her father and at herself. She wondered what her mother would have been like if things had worked out with that other man. Would she have been a more joyful person, a more encouraging person? Maybe, but maybe not. It was hard to tell, because her mother was her mother, and she was not like April.

"All right then, I have to go now," April said quietly.

"April, are you all right?"

"Yes, Mom, I'm fine. I love you."

"Love you, too," her mother mumbled. It had always been hard for her to say the words.

But she was not like her mother, April reminded herself again after she hung up the phone.

Maybe her mother had made the right choices for *her* life.

"But this life is mine," April whispered. Could she settle for a man like Greg who would be kind and intelligent, but would never inspire joy and passion?

The answer was obvious. She didn't love Greg.

She loved Dylan, even though she could never have him. He'd showed her the value of love, in the way he'd had to live without it, and in the way he'd faced his fears of closeness in order to make his brothers feel safe and wanted. He'd helped her get past her own fears of being able to love a child again, and he'd shown her that finding a good man who shared her interests wasn't enough when there was no love in her heart. He'd even rid her life of Jason Olney.

So what would she do now?

"Maybe I'll spend my life finding perfect matches for other people," she murmured, looking at her computer screen. Or maybe she'd just delete this silly program.

The doorbell rang before she could make a decision.

She looked at the clock and frowned. Eight o'clock in the morning?

Carefully, she glanced out the peephole. Peering out, she saw Dylan standing there. Farther back at the end of her drive was a Valentine Enterprises truck.

She swung the door open in a wide arc.

"Dylan?"

He smiled. "Bet you're wondering why I'm here, but don't worry. I haven't come to ask you to help me out of a bind again."

That was too bad. She stepped aside to let him in. Right now she would welcome a chance to start over with him. Any chance. Any task. But he didn't have a job for her.

"Dylan, why *are* you here? I thought you would have been getting ready to leave town already. Did your business trip overseas fall through? Is something wrong? Is it the boys?" Suddenly her heart caught in her throat. What if he'd been trying to call while she'd been on the phone to her mother or online? Something must be wrong.

He placed gentle hands on her shoulders and shook his head. "Shh, the boys are fine. I'm rethinking the trip overseas, and I'm here to... Well, the thing is that I've been worried about you since you've been gone. I know how you tend to stick your nose in a textbook or get on your computer and forget everything else, like locking your doors properly," he said with a frown, indicating the fact that she had let him inside without throwing the deadbolt or unlatching a chain.

She felt a warm blush creeping up her throat. She *had* been preoccupied since she'd been home, but books or computers hadn't had anything to do with it.

"I'll try to remember," she promised lamely.

He raised a hand as if to touch her cheek, then let it fall. "Yes, well," he said, his voice low and thick. "I'm sure you'll mean to, but I'm in the business of security systems, after all. I thought I'd just do my part to help ensure your safety. I hope you won't mind if I take the initiative and install a safety net in your house, a system so that you won't have to worry if you lose track of what's going on. You'll be safe with or without being conscious of it."

"Dylan," she said slowly, staring up into his intense eyes. "You don't have to do that. I'll be fine. Don't worry."

"Too late. I'm already worried," he said in that low, sexy drawl.

"But this is an expensive system."

"I can afford it."

"You don't owe me anything, Dylan. You don't have to do this for me."

"Then let me do it for *me*. April, do you think I'm going to sleep well at night wondering if you're safe?"

"Dylan, I'm always safe," she tried to say with a shaky laugh.

He didn't answer, just looked at her with those soulful eyes, and she was reminded that the first time she met him, she was being harassed by a man. Not exactly safe.

"I, well, I guess I wouldn't want you to lose sleep."

He took a step toward her, and she caught her breath. "That's very good then, because I have been, you know," he said. "I didn't sleep at all last night. How about you? Were you okay last night?"

She hadn't slept, either. Not a second.

"I'm…having some trouble adjusting," she admitted. She wasn't going to admit that she was missing him desperately. That wouldn't be fair to him. "Why are you rethinking your trip overseas?"

He shook his head. "Like I said, I've been worried about you. How could I go, not knowing if you were safe? Will you… Would you let me…"

Touch me, she wanted to beg. *Kiss me. Love me.* But of course, she couldn't say that. She knew love wasn't something he was interested in.

"Dylan?" The word came out on a breath. She tipped her head back so that she could look into his eyes more fully. For a minute she thought he was going to kiss her. Then he shook his head and glanced toward her computer. A frown drew his brows together.

"It would be a great favor to me if you'd let me install

a Valentine system,'' he said. ''Maybe then I'd worry less. Perhaps I could even sleep at night.''

And she remembered how he'd taken on the care of those less able to look after themselves than he was. Like Sam and Jordie. He was still fighting bullies and his past, remembering that he hadn't felt safe and struggling to change that for others. She knew his past still haunted him, and all of this was tied up with things that had happened long ago. She didn't want him to be thinking about her just because he was worried about her. She didn't need a protector or a superhero. She needed love, but that wasn't something he could supply.

And she could ease his mind.

''That would be wonderful,'' she finally said. ''Thank you for caring. I can probably pay you back over time.''

He cast a murderous look her way. ''Don't even think about it.''

She opened her mouth to object, and he raised one dangerous brow.

''To take money for what I've offered and can supply so easily would be an insult,'' he said simply.

She shut her mouth. ''All right.''

He stared at her long and hard, then he went outside. When he returned, he was carrying what looked like an oversize briefcase. ''I've sent my men to work on the garage. I'll see to the controls. If you don't mind, we'll use your computer. I'll tie things in here so that when we're done, you can turn things on and off from various places, including the computer. You won't have to in-terrupt your work.''

She nodded as he sat down at her computer and

opened his case. Clearly he knew his stuff, as he stopped to ask her questions now and then as he worked.

"How's…Greg? Have you heard from him?" he asked.

Greg doesn't matter, she wanted to cry. Only you matter. "We've talked online," she admitted. "We've agreed that we don't suit."

He looked up at that, over the top of her computer. His golden eyes met hers in a long, unreadable look.

"Then you're still looking for your perfect mate," he said, glancing down at the screen of her computer. His voice almost felt like a caress. When he said the word "mate," she felt a bit faint.

For long seconds, she said nothing. Then she slowly shook her head. "No, I'm not looking any longer."

Dylan raised his head suddenly. "You've found someone else, then?"

The room seemed to vibrate with the question. April knew that she should say "Yes." It would keep him from finding out the truth. When he'd installed this system, he would go and never worry about her again, but if he thought she was floundering, searching for what could never be, he might worry. He might call occasionally to check up on her. It would be torture, dragging things out that way, always waiting for the phone to ring, just so she could hear his voice. She should definitely lie to him, but this was Dylan.

She realized that she was staring straight into his eyes, and that all the love and longing she was feeling for him were probably right there in her eyes where it could hurt him.

She looked away…and realized she just couldn't lie to him. "It was a foolish system," she said, picking up a pencil she found on the coffee table. "I guess I've decided that you can't really choose a husband scientifically. There has to be more."

"So you're not looking for a husband anymore at all."

She shook her head sadly.

The silence in the room stretched out. Unbearably long.

When she finally looked up, Dylan was still staring at her. He didn't look calm.

"Dylan?" She choked out the word, rising from her seat and walking toward him.

"I'm sorry," he said, standing to meet her. "I'm sorry to hear that you don't believe in making matches any more. I'll admit that I'm not here just to install a security system for you. I've... April, I've made a decision. I don't want to go to Europe alone. You've had such an effect on me and you've made me realize that I'm not getting any younger, that life is passing me by. I'm, well, I've decided to follow your lead. I'm thinking of marrying, after all. I was thinking that maybe you could help me find the perfect woman. We could use your system, see how it works." He held out his hand, and folded her fingers into his gentle grasp. He gave a slight tug and drew her toward the computer.

He was thinking of getting married. He was thinking of getting married. He was thinking of getting married. Because of what she'd shown him and all she'd done with Greg. Now she was going to have to watch him choose a woman made just for him. A debutante, no doubt, someone worthy of a Valentine, someone beautiful, poised, sophisticated, raised on the North shore. His perfect woman.

April's throat closed off. Tears stung the backs of her eyes.

Dylan was looking at her so hopefully. He wanted her to find the right woman for him. She couldn't do it. She didn't want to do it. He'd have no trouble finding tons of candidates if all he did was whisper his intentions on the wind. Women would line up outside his door. He'd have his pick. No machinery needed.

"April? Sweetheart?" Dylan was drawing her in, looking at her with worried eyes.

"I... Dylan, I—" She couldn't keep staring into his eyes. Her heart was breaking, shattering into pieces. She had to get out of here, and so she looked away. Down.

Her gaze skimmed across the computer screen, slipped away, then came back.

The page on the screen was familiar. It had nothing to do with a security system. She knew that page, that program. She'd written it.

He'd pulled up her program. No, he'd changed her program.

"Dylan?" On the screen in front of her were two photos, herself and Dylan. A perfect match, the computer told her.

It was too much. The hot tears were threatening. She tried to raise her chin and look up at him, but she couldn't see him through the blur of mist that shrouded her vision. Her lips trembled, and she feared she would never find her voice.

"I'm...I'm sure there's some mistake. No computer

program would ever consider us a scientific match," she managed to say, though her throat ached.

Dylan practically growled. "I don't give a damn if we're a scientific match," he said. "We're a match in every other way, and I don't need a computer program to verify that. I know it in my soul."

She blinked and the mist cleared enough for her to see his beautiful eyes. "Dylan, do you know what you're saying? Have you really thought this through?"

"You mean, am I going to be like dear old dad or the men you've known before me? Am I going to change my mind once you're pregnant? April, love," he said, dropping to his knees before her. "You've shown me so much these past few weeks. I've discovered things about myself that I would never have known without you. I've just found out that I have a heart and the ability to feel things deeply. And this heart is working just fine, April. Just perfectly, because I love you, sweetheart. Even one night away from you nearly killed me. I miss you. Already. So much."

He glanced to the side at the computer screen. "I know how it is. A computer wouldn't really ever match us up, but I hope you'll consider me, even though I don't meet your requirements for a husband. And in spite of the fact that I tricked you and messed with your computer program. I love you, angel. So much. I'm sorry if I've upset you."

But the words were barely out of his mouth when April slipped to the floor beside him. She wrapped her arms around his neck and pressed her lips to his. When she finally pulled back, silent tears of joy had slipped down her face.

"You meet all my requirements," she said, her voice choked. "You're all I want, all I love. Who needs a computer to tell me that?"

And she turned in his arms and clicked off her computer.

A shrill alarm began shrieking throughout her house. April jerked in Dylan's arms. She stared at him wide-eyed. Obviously he *had* been working on a security system.

"Oh dear, it looks like I've set something off," she said.

"Oh, yes," he said, pulling her closer against his heart. "You've very definitely set something off." He reached down and shut off the system he'd set up.

Quiet filled the room, and a world of meaning was in Dylan's eyes.

He touched his lips to hers. "From the day I met you," he said, dropping numerous kisses on her lips, trailing down to her jaw. "You've been setting off alarms in my head."

She swallowed hard as his mouth found the pulse point in her throat.

"That—that doesn't sound good," she managed to whisper hoarsely.

He pulled back and smiled at her. "Oh, that's very good, sweetheart. I love the sound of alarms. They're my business, they're in my blood. *You're* in my blood, and I'm desperately hoping that you'll agree to be my wife, because there's nothing I want more than to be your husband and to someday be a father again. A real one this time."

She frowned at that. "You were very real to the boys," she said, resting her hands on his chest. She could feel his heartbeat thundering beneath her fingertips. "I hope you'll stay in their lives as much as possible."

"I wouldn't miss it. Besides, Sam and Jordie and I share a secret. We all love you."

April felt as if she'd just swallowed a star. "How could I ever have thought there was any man for me but you?"

"Well, I intend to spend my life proving to you that we were made for each other. I want to be the man you write about in your journal."

She rested her lips against his, lightly, not allowing herself more yet. "I have a secret. I think you always were the man in my journal. You're the man I always wanted, the man I want to be the father to my children."

He took her lips in a long kiss, then pulled back and tucked his fingertips beneath her chin. "That sounds like a wonderful story. I can't wait to read the rest of it."

"I can't wait to live the rest of it," she said on a whisper.

"Then let's not wait," he said, and his lips came down on hers as they began the story of a match that couldn't be more perfect.

* * * * *

Chapter One

Kate slipped her hands into the folds of her skirt to keep anyone from noticing that her fingers were trembling. She hated putting herself on display this way, but heck, she'd meant every word she'd said about Safe House. Those kids were more important than her fears. Still, her fears were very real. They were being fueled by that tall, lean man with the golden-brown hair and the soot-gray suit that cost more than her entire wardrobe. A dream man, most women would say.

The worst kind of man for a woman like her.

Dreams were dangerous. Reality was so much better. Safer. Ryerson women were known for being suckers for dreams that took over their lives and ruined their worlds. Fortunately, she was the one Ryerson who had successfully bucked tradition. She wasn't going to risk failure now.

Still, it was difficult to ignore a man so gorgeous. Especially when he was examining her as if he knew just what she looked like when she slipped between the sheets at night.

Her breath caught in her throat, her cheeks felt unaccountably warm. Completely irresponsible to be imagining such things. She looked away and tried to concentrate on her reason for being here as Donnie read her qualifications.

"Please let a woman hire me," she whispered beneath her breath. Not that she hadn't had successful work relationships with men before. Just not lately. She didn't want to deal with the possible complications.

But fervent thought just wasn't enough, because thirty seconds into the bidding, the golden-brown-haired man glanced up at her and moved nearer the stage.

"Fifteen thousand dollars," the man said, in a deep, quiet voice. His lazy smile had half the women in the audience turning their attention from the auction block to the man.

Kate's nerves felt as if they were trembling as much as her hands. But she'd learned from years of nursing that a steady expression and a take-no-prisoners tone of voice could work wonders with most people.

"Excuse me, sir, but you don't look like you need a nurse," she said, staring directly into the eyes that could convince the most chaste woman to shimmy out of her underwear.

"You don't look like most nurses I've met," he replied with a glance that sent a delicious wicked shiver straight down her body. Kate took a deep breath to chase away her reaction. The man was obviously used to getting his way with women.

"Just because I'm not dressed for the part doesn't mean I'm not a nurse."

"And just because a person's wounds aren't visible doesn't mean they aren't there," he answered softly.

Touché. She knew that better than anyone. She nodded. "You're right. I'm sorry. You do need a nurse, then?"

He shook his head slowly. "Not at all."

Uh-oh. What did he need?

Donnie, the auctioneer, looked around. "Anyone bid more than fifteen thousand?"

Kate knew it was too much to hope for, but she also knew that working for that gorgeous man with the velvet voice and the I-can-make-you-sigh eyes was just going to be a nightmare.

"Going once," Donnie said.

Kate felt an urge to plead with the audience, to name off her qualifications all over again, to stress what an asset she would be for a family or a sweet little old lady.

Of course she didn't, and when she stole a glance at her bidder, she thought she saw sympathy in his gaze.

"Going twice," Donnie said.

The man might have felt sympathy, but he didn't withdraw his bid.

"Sold to the man in the gray suit," Donnie said.

Kate took a deep breath. So be it. She had been hired. She was a professional. She would do whatever job this man had hired her for, so long as it was respectable.

Slowly she came halfway down the risers as her new employer stepped up until she was only one stair above him. Still, she had to tip her head back slightly to stare into his eyes. He was close enough that she could breathe in the scent of musk and soap and man. His shoulders were so broad that she could not see past him on either side.

"I don't understand," she said tentatively. "You said

you didn't really need a nurse, but that was an awful lot of money to bid."

"I didn't lie. I don't need a nurse. And I bid a great deal because I can and because I'm going to ask a great deal of you. More than you may feel comfortable giving."

Her heart began to pound fast. She knew that her eyes had probably grown alarmingly large. Kate hoped that she didn't look frightened. As a nurse, she'd learned to disguise fear even when fear was justified, but this was a different kind of fear than she was used to.

"What...what are you looking for?"

He smiled then, and yes, his smile was kind. "I'm looking for a bride-to-be, Ms. Ryerson."

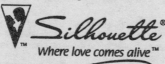

If you enjoyed what you just read,
then we've got an offer you can't resist!

Take 2 bestselling love stories FREE!

Plus get a FREE surprise gift!

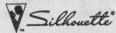

COMING NEXT MONTH

#1624 SKY FULL OF PROMISE—Teresa Southwick
The Coltons
Dr. Dominic Rodriguez's fiancée ran out on him—and it was all Sky Colton's fault! Feeling guilty about the breakup, Sky reluctantly posed as Dom's finacée to calm his frazzled mother. But would their pretend engagement lead to a real marriage proposal?

#1625 HIS BEST FRIEND'S BRIDE—Jodi O'Donnell
Bridgewater Bachelors
Born in the same hospital on the same day, Julia Sennett, Griff Corbin and Reb Farley were best friends—until romance strained their bonds. Engaged to Reb, Julia questioned her choice in future husbands. Now Griff must choose between his childhood buddy...and the woman he loves!

#1626 STRANDED WITH SANTA—Janet Tronstad
Wealthy, successful rodeo cowboy Zack Lucas hated Christmas—he didn't want to be a mail-carrying Santa and he certainly didn't want to fall in love with Jenny Collins. But a brutal Montana storm left Zach snowbound on his mail route, which meant spending the holidays in Jenny's arms...!

#1627 THE BARON & THE BODYGUARD—Valerie Parv
The Carramer Legacy
Stricken with amnesia, Mathiaz de Marigny didn't remember telling his beautiful bodyguard that he loved her—or that she had refused him. Now Jacinta Newnham vowed a new start between them. But what would happen when the truth surrounding Mathiaz's accident—and Jacinta's connection to it—surfaced?

#1628 HER LAST CHANCE—DeAnna Talcott
Soulmates
Looking for a spirited filly with unicorn blood, foreign heiress Mallory Chevalle found no-nonsense horse breeder Chase Wells. According to legend, his special horse could heal her ailing father and restore harmony to her homeland. But could a love-smitten Mallory heal Chase's wounded heart?

#1629 CHRISTMAS DUE DATE—Moyra Tarling
Mac Kingston was a loner who hadn't counted on sharing the holidays—or his inheritance—with very beautiful, very wary and very pregnant Eve Darling. But when she realized she'd found the perfect father—and husband!—could she convince Mac?

SRCNM1002